Defiant Little Bubbles of Joy

A Razor Wit Book by

Piet Marino

Cover design: samarapowers.com

ISBN-13:979-8-9854917-4-6

pietmarino.com

Many thanks to those who guided this book from its origins and evolving titles (*Fago, Magic and Misery*, to name a couple) to its current state: Laura Albert, Aaron Broadwell, Kathy Cheney, Tom Ecobelli, Kathy Herold, Regina Griffin, Courtney Reid, Bill Reiss, and Nancy Seid.

Chapter 1

"Fago is a hard emotion to explain," Mrs. Burrell, our English-11 teacher had told us. "It's from a tribe in the Pacific Islands. It means feeling both affection and worry for someone at the same time. You might feel fago for someone whose job can put them in danger—a firefighter, for example."

It intrigued me to learn there was an emotion I'd never heard of. Later, when Pan was gone, I realized that was definitely what I had felt for him. The first time I saw him—not interacting with anyone, his elegance so out of place in our classroom—I felt enchanted, but worried. Because as radiant and confident as he came across, it couldn't have been easy transferring into a new school in November. And there was just the slightest something about his face, a pinpoint betrayal of sadness or vulnerability or longing, I'm not sure.

He was probably the most beautiful person I'd ever seen, and while that may not be saying a lot in Mungers Mills, in any location it would have been true. I watched him, and sometimes he would catch me and give me a quick smile. But he stayed completely to himself those first weeks. There were rumors about him, all dumb, and I think people eventually forgot about this new, tall boy who didn't say much.

He even sat in the cafeteria alone, at a small, square table right in my line of sight from where I sat with Amanda. I kept wanting to invite him over, and if I'd had more confidence, I would have. Still, he appeared content to be by himself.

I knew what it was like to be the new kid. At the end of the first day of ninth grade, over two years ago, the bunch of us Holy Redeemer girls—me, Amanda, Mary, Emma, Sandy—had all huddled at the high school's front entrance for comfort, and to compare stories about this new world of public school. It was so big to us then—more than one hallway—and there were strange faces and the constant reality that everyone who had gone to the public middle school together was summing us up. Now that I was a junior, it was hard to remember that I had once considered this place huge or affluent or the least bit sophisticated.

Our principal, Dr. Jackson, had the annoying habit of revealing birthdays at the end of the morning newscast. People cringed when homeroom rang out with the birthday song. Even the student anchors looked like they hated it, and on November 28 it was my turn. But I had a cringe buddy because it turned out to be Pan's birthday too.

"I should go say something to him," I said to Amanda during lunch, sneaking another glance. He looked the same as always, not uncomfortable in solitude. But knowing it was his birthday made his solitude unbearable for me—and gave me an excuse to approach him.

"Do it," Amanda said. "He's really cute. Better than cute. Try to find out if he has a girlfriend."

"That would be the last thing I'd ever do," I said.

"Nia," she said, "get over yourself. The only one who thinks you're not pretty is you. So get over there and meet that hot guy."

"I'm just going to say hi, to be friendly," I said, standing. "No one should eat alone on their birthday."

"Maybe he can be more than a friend," she said too loud. I waved her off.

I might as well have been about to ask him to marry me the way I was trembling as I approached.

"Happy birthday," I said. "I guess."

He hadn't looked up at me until I started to speak, and I was sure this was going to be even more humiliating than I was prepared for. Then he smiled, and it seemed genuine.

"Sit," he said, pointing to the chair across from him. "We need to celebrate."

"Why don't you come sit with us?" I asked. "My friend Amanda's over there waiting." He smiled again, then picked up his stuff and followed me. I had never felt so self-conscious in the cafeteria before, and never so elated.

"Any free seats?" he asked when he got to our table. He had this rich, smooth tone that was way older than a teenage voice, more like James Bond. Amanda looked up as if she were staring into the sun. She pointed to one of the two empty chairs.

"Thanks." He took the one next to me. "If you sit alone for more than two weeks, they assume you're going to shoot up the school."

"You're not, are you?" Amanda asked, smile blazing.

"Nope, I'm totally ammo-free. I don't even carry a comb."

I tried not to stare at him, and at the same time tried not to avoid eye contact. Those eyes demanded contact. They were a piercing green. I was not going to survive this meal.

Trying to pull myself together, I commented on the fact

that we'd all brought our lunches.

"My mother is completely organic," he said, "as well as a teensy bit insane. She packs mine for me."

"I make my own," said Amanda. "Always have. Just a habit by now."

"Yeah," I said. "My mom's sandwiches are better than school food."

"Anything is," Pan said.

"Yeah." I didn't mention that the reason I brought it was I didn't have the money to buy, and there was no way I was applying for free or reduced lunch. Maybe I should have said so because the conversation dried up. If Pan was disturbed by the ensuing silence, he didn't look it, just kept eating. When I didn't think I could stand it another second, he said, "Happy birthday. To us." He opened the lid of a square plastic food saver, revealing a huge wedge of unfrosted chocolate cake, which he took a plastic knife to. His willowy, strong fingers worked like a surgeon's. He placed one piece next to my sandwich and one next to Amanda's, no discussion. I was glad, too, because I would have felt obliged to decline if he'd asked first, and it was incredible.

"Mother made this," he said. "Organic. All natural ingredients. And still somehow flavorful."

This was maybe what chocolate originally tasted like, when it needed only a little sugar rather than a crate. It was ripe and fresh and full, and I immediately wanted what was left of theirs, maybe the whole cake if I could find out where this guy lived.

"Good, right?" he asked.

"Yes, um ...." I said.

"Excellent," said Amanda.

"And not one insect was harmed in its production."

The cake must have contained some kind of relaxing agent

because I immediately felt like we were all friends now. This most gorgeous boy had not rejected me—he was feeding me.

"We're both late babies," I said.

"Yeah," said Amanda. "You guys should be seniors."

"My parents held me back because they thought I wasn't ready for school," he said. "Which is amazing, since they can't wait to get rid of me now."

"My mom thought I wasn't social enough to start school," I said, "so she kept me home. Back then she liked the company. But with my baby brother, she wants him to start kindergarten as soon as he can walk."

I collected crumbs with my thumb and tried not to look too hoggish getting them into my mouth.

"This is so good," I said.

"It could bring you to tears," said Amanda.

"There's plenty more where that came from," Pan said. "But you'll have to come to my house for it."

Somehow I knew that he was not inviting either of us as a date, that this was as innocent as Amanda inviting me over. Still, it was thrilling.

"Happy seventeenth." He held up his juice bottle. Amanda and I held up our milk cartons and we toasted.

"I guess we're the class elders," he said to me, smiling, and showing that peephole of longing.

~

Pan sat with us at lunch from then on, which was a daily thrill. It wasn't just the rippling, very blond hair he adamantly denied lightening when Amanda asked him outright. He had the body, too. It wasn't the pumped-up, dieted-down-to-no-fat look or the steroidal deformation. Pan was a tennis player—or had been at his last school—and he had a natural, lithe shape. And don't make me think about those legs. Our gym classes were coed, and the first time I saw him in shorts, I felt like I was high on nighttime cough syrup. That's it, I thought. I'll pass out into his arms. When I wake up, we will be in love forever.

I didn't faint on him, although I imagined every strategy and gimmick possible for making bodily contact, to make it clear that I was available for deep friendship leading to intense romance. I don't know what gave me the spirit to flirt with him, since it had never worked with any other boy. I hoped that if he had no interest in me—like all the rest—he would wait awhile, not rush reality.

I started to entertain—too intensely—a fantasy life with Pan. I had it all planned out, which is a little sad in retrospect. First of all, he would realize his attraction to stout, sturdy girls and not be able to stay away from me. Next would be our higher education. I couldn't get into Harvard like he could, since, as it turned out, he was also genetically smart, and was taking the only two honors courses our school had to offer. Hard classes like chemistry and math were like swinging a tennis racket for him. I would have to forge my college plans around his because we couldn't have a commuter relationship. I wouldn't want him falling in love with some other strapping Italian babe with an inordinate amount of arm hair. I could get into someplace a little less competitive than the Ivy Leagues, maybe a state school nearby. Finances would be tough, but I was used to having no money. We'd make the sacrifices for four years, and then Pan would go to medical school or law school while I worked at my new career. It would all pay off, with both of us making so much money that eventually I could work part-time while we raised our beautiful children. We wouldn't consider signing a prenuptial agreement, since in this fantasy we would stay together forever and always be in love despite being married before we were old enough to drink.

It was in Science and Society with Mrs. Mercado that Pan burst this fantasy dead. She was telling us something about domestic abuse statistics and made a related reference to "the LGBTQ+ community." Mrs. Mercado was not the kind of teacher kids fooled around with, but there was no missing the whispered comments from Patrick Torno and Boz Samson when she said this. I looked over at my new friend, embarrassed that he had to see what kind of idiots we harbored here, and saw that he stiffened, lowered his eyelids a little. Then he said what I'm sure no person at Mungers Mills High School ever had.

"If one-tenth of the world is queer, I'm the fraction in this class."

The stillness in the room was like waiting for a piece of an iceberg to collapse. Amy Conrad, another girl I'd known from Holy Redeemer, folded her hands and looked more sour than usual.

Finally, Mrs. Mercado smiled and said to Pan, "I think that's the bravest thing I've ever heard. If you're being serious."

"No reason not to be," he said.

Chapter 2

The disappointment had such a stranglehold on me that I couldn't look at him the rest of the class. I avoided him after the bell and left the building when school let out without making eye contact with anyone. Maybe I had known in some recess of my brain, and that's why I'd had the nerve to talk to him at all. Maybe that's why I had been bold enough to fantasize about him.

Pan called me that night. If he had called me the night before, I would have been orbiting the earth. But now I was numb.

"Hi," he said. "You looked upset, and I—"

"Why did you have to tell me?" I blurted.

"I'm sorry."

"It's just that—"

"Forget I said anything," he said. "It's not true. I was running lines for a play."

"No, no, no, I don't mean that."

"Then why are you so mad?"

"I'm not mad," I said, which was true, being more like devastated. And in that state I was having trouble controlling my mouth. "I wanted to think you weren't gay so I could dream about us getting married someday." There was nothing on the other end, which was to be expected after such a ridiculous outburst. I would never be able to go to school again after saying that.

But then he said, "We could get married, if you want. We've got a week off at Christmas."

I laughed, almost hysterically, and tears came pouring out.

When I had calmed down a little, he said, "We might as well. It's not like many guys are knocking on my door in this town."

I wiped my eyes, blew my nose. "That's what every girl wants to hear. 'I'll marry you if a better guy doesn't come along.'"

"That's not what I meant."

"Why couldn't you at least hold off until graduation? Let a girl have some hope."

"I could go through reparative therapy."

"What's that?"

"They show you pictures of sweaty bodybuilders and then zap your gonads. Boner derailed."

"For good."

"I won't know until I try. Okay, here, I've got some wires. I'll hook them up now, and ...." He did something in the background, then let out a howl.

I didn't want to laugh again but couldn't help it. "Are you straight yet?" I asked.

"My hair is."

"I knew it wouldn't work. Nothing works for me."

"I'm sorry. Again."

"Why couldn't you just pretend, you know, like other boys do when the rumors start?"

"That was inconsiderate," he said. "But there are some

things you have to share with your only friend. Your dreams, your goals. Especially your goal of meeting the right boy someday."

"My entire love life is set in fantasy. Now I have to face reality again. I've had enough reality in my life."

"I'm sorry. I'm a dud."

"No, I'm the dud," I said. "That's been proven."

"You're not, Nia. Nowhere near."

"A girl who's seventeen and never even had a date?"

"There's nothing wrong with you. You're just leading an alternative lifestyle."

"If you're going to be so handsome, you need to expect a few straight girls to go crazy for you. Especially the plain ones."

"I don't see plain. I see an Italian princess."

"That's not a compliment where I come from."

"Do you want to fight about who's the bigger loser?" he asked.

"It'll give me some time to get over my disappointment," I said, though even as the words came out I was getting tired of the self-pity. I cleared my throat. "Anyway, I thought it was brave, telling the whole class that way."

"Really?"

"Really."

"Because it got so quiet I might as well have said I was Osama bin Laden's water boy."

"Yeah, you even shut up Boz Samson for a few seconds."

"He's a piece of work. And what's with his friend, slouched in his seat like he has no spine. Is that some yoga position?"

"That's Patrick Torno. He scares me a little."

"Speaking of scary, this is the only school of the many I've attended that doesn't have a GSA. Not even a barely functioning one."

"GSA? Gay something? I don't know the rest."

"Genders & Sexualities Alliance."

"Would you go if there was one?"

"I'd be sitting by myself, wouldn't I? Unless Boz and Torno dropped in to lend their support."

"I don't want to talk about them. I'm still mourning my lost prom date. I had such a great night planned for us, too. Dinner, then the dance, then ...."

"Then great sex?"

"First sex, in my case. And I wouldn't care if it was great."

"What's the problem? I can still be your date. There's not like a homo screening at the door, right? I can't imagine Mungers Mills has that kind of technology. Will I have to wear a tux?"

"I can wear the tux if you want." I sighed. It would save me from doing a waxing that day.

"You wear a nice dress and I'll wear a nice tux, and we'll be the prettiest people there."

"Well ...."

"Is it a deal, Nia? We are officially prom dates?"

"Do you swear it wasn't the thought of dating me that scared you out of the closet?"

"I'm serious," he said.

"In that case," I said, "I have a few conditions."

"Let me guess: You want to go in a limousine, not a dump truck like everyone else here. Easy enough."

"No, but you are not allowed to be the best dancer in the place. I know that's a stereotype and all, but just in case."

"That will be hard. I used to be in a boy band."

"Second, you may have to ugly yourself up for the evening."

"That'll be even harder."

"Work on it. Tone down the radiance."

"Radiance?"

"I don't want people so blinded that they don't see me at all."

"I won't take a shower or brush my hair. For days."

"That ought to do it," I said. "Well, this has been one unusual conversation. But I should get going on my homework."

"Okay," he said. "Now don't conveniently forget about our prom date. The only deal breaker will be if you find a real guy between now and then. Which is easily possible because you are pretty and perfect."

"Sure. Goodnight."

"Sleep tight. Loves ya."

"Loves ya?"

"Yeah, you know, when you're too shy to conjugate the verb? Loves ya."

"I see. Loves you," I said. "That doesn't exactly roll off my tongue."

"It will."

In reality, people would snicker at us for our arrangement, but too bad for them. My date might not want to kiss me passionately, but I would have the best-looking one.

Amanda called me right after to discuss Pan's announcement in class, but I had no interest. I did manage to tell her about the prom.

"This could be viewed as progress," I said. "It's only December and I actually have a date for a dance five months away."

Chapter 3

Ironically, Pan may have slid into the best-friend slot because he revealed why he was yet another boy who would not be my boyfriend. Or maybe it was his story about his real dad. Or the story about his mom pulling him out of Buckingham Heights because she couldn't stand suburbia anymore, which was not their first move. Or that we both loved to walk, at a time in our lives when everyone else was driving like they had invented it. Or our mutual love of big, splashy movies, which he took me to in Holland Park, where they had an actual multiplex. Or the fact that from then on he called me every night to catch up on whatever he might have missed since the final bell. He loved talking on the phone and never texted, as if that were beneath him. He didn't seem to care if I was half-asleep already when he called, or on the toilet. Of course, I would have had to explain why I had my phone with me in the bathroom, so I didn't complain.

Maybe it was because I had stopped hanging around in groups after ninth grade. My old group, the Holy Redeemer transplants, had long since assimilated. We were still friends, and I still felt the old bond with them. But somehow, between then and now, the schedule of my life had gotten complicated, leaving me with no energy to go out at night. Because of homework, babysitting my brother Paolo, and my job at the pharmacy, I usually saw my friends only in school. Otherwise, it was phone friendship. Amanda and Pan were among the few people I spoke to in real time outside those walls.

Amanda was short and kind of round. She smiled all the time, her big cheeks swelling up, but not so much that they detracted from the animation in her eyes. She was the easiest friend a person could ask for, but she—like everyone else— was more into socializing than I was. She was always bubbling about an upcoming dance or the bonfire before a big football game on a Friday night. But Friday mornings I would wake up and think about the full day of school, then about doing an hour or so with Paolo and some housework, then going to work until nine. Imagining going out after all that and getting home late, only to have to get up early to work again made me want to crawl back into bed. So I had given up on Friday nights. Eventually, Saturday nights got away from me as well.

Amanda and I always had lunch together, and now that Pan had come out, she was back to talking about the topic she liked best—boys. She focused on males elsewhere—TV, Internet, movies, the mall in Holland Park—because there was only so much you could say about the local boys. When we had first started at MMHS, it had been the land of tall men, so far out of reach we could only dream about them. But now that we were older and our eyes were more open, we could see that so many of them were fuzzy and zitty and, worst, not into grooming. The boys in Mungers Mills wore baseball caps as if they'd been born with them on. Probably they wore them to bed. Once I saw an irritated Eucharistic Minister at church take a boy's hat off and hand it to him before giving him communion.

Amanda had the same issue with romance that I did: always longing. But she was willing to take risks, while I was waiting for someone to discover me. Because of her drive, she did have dates here and there, and even a boyfriend for a few weeks. But each time the guy hinted he was looking for someone else, someone unlike her, a girl who wasn't short and round and giggly.

It was becoming clear that Pan neither liked nor disliked Amanda. He was polite and attentive to her, but even though he liked boys the way that she did, he didn't find her constant stream interesting. Maybe what finally clinched our best-friendship was that Amanda's lunch mod got changed when she made All County Chorus and had rehearsals in the middle of the day.

Pan's and my non-romance progressed so fast that before long I was someone he could say pretty much anything to, someone he could arm-wrestle with and lose, the brother he'd never had. He even called me Bro for a while. And I did feel different with Pan than I had with my other friends. I once heard that if you hung around with smart people, you got smarter. The same must be true about other traits because in trying to keep up with Pan, I was more glib and more sarcastic. Usually I tended to be polite and deferential, but with him the naughty girl came out to play. I enjoyed her.

For instance, you might be thinking his name was Pan because he looked like some Greek god with a flute, minus the goat hooves. But his real name was James, and Pan was short for Pansy because after Pan made his little revelation, Boz Samson called him that.

"That's the best he can come up with?" Pan asked me later, almost bewildered. "With all the gay slurs to choose from? Pansy?" So we co-opted and cropped it and James was renamed.

"I like it," he had said. "Kind of subversive."

The story of my own name was not rooted in protest. It started with my older brother, Teo. My dad regretted not having named him after himself—Anthony—right up to the day I was born four years later. Since I turned out to be a girl and Teo had gotten used to his name by then, my parents had settled on Antonia, the Italian female form of Anthony. They gave me Mom's name for the middle, JoAnne. Antonia JoAnne Fazzino didn't have a flow to it. And since neither of my parents had the patience for a lot of syllables, I became Toni. However, since Tony was my dad's nickname, they started calling me AJ. It was efficient, and technically correct, and, like so many things in my life, not decorative. I always hated it, and by the time I knew my letters, I decided I deserved more of them. Besides, people kept mistaking AJ for a boy, which was a huge deal for a five-year-old girl. I carried on quite a bit, which was unusual for me, being otherwise compliant. So Mom and I spent a lot of time looking at my full name spelled out in big crayon letters, searching for alternatives. One day she simply cleaved off the last three letters of my first name and I became Nia, which I really liked. According to Mom, I was quite assertive about enforcing this new name, especially with my older brother who behaved like older brothers do. And I was vigilant with people who said Mia instead, correcting them with polite insistence. Ultimately the world around me forgot AJ and I had the pretty and melodious name I deserved.

Incidentally, when Mom and Dad became parents one more time, sixteen years after I was born, they must have been too worn out to remember that Dad had wanted a male namesake, and they called my baby brother Paolo.

Chapter 4

I was a stock person and cashier at Polaski's Pharmacy on Broad Street, which used to be the main shopping area in town. There was never enough time between when school got out and when I needed to be at work, but Pan insisted that I meet his family. He lived with his mom and his stepdad, and his grandmother. So, one Friday after school he took me to his house.

"I have to warn you about Gram," he said. "She's been dying for thirty-one years. I believe her meanness is preserving her, like brine. One day she'll like you and the next day she won't like anyone."

"Which day is today?" I asked.

"Not sure. It depends on which way her blood is flowing."

He was wrong. Her mood shifted much faster than every twenty-four hours. When we walked in the front door of their gigantic house, she smiled like she was recognizing an old friend. I felt sure she was just a sweet old lady, a typical grandmother sitting in a broiling living room. She was dressed in a white blouse with a high neck and long sleeves, and black pants. She held a cane, which was pointed at the floor even though she was sitting.

"Gram, this is Nia."

"Nia?" she asked, still smiling.

"Yes, nice to meet you," I said.

"Nia?" she asked again.

"Yes. How are you?"

"What kind of name is that?"

"Sorry?"

"*Nia* is a sound a baby would make. *Neeeaahhh.*"

"Gram," Pan said.

"What kind of name? It's a polite question."

"If it were a polite question, you wouldn't be asking it."

"Why didn't they name her something that sounds like a name?"

"It's a nickname. A girl's nickname. Now be nice."

She looked at me, her eyes trying to bore into my head. "Are you here looking for money?"

"What?" I asked, taking a step back.

"Gram, that's enough."

"I want James to date a real girl. Not an imposter, a swindler."

"Okay, Grandmother. You've terrorized enough children for one day. We have to go."

Pan took me by the arm and led me toward a lustrous oak staircase. I couldn't help glancing back at the old woman, as if she would take back her accusations if I looked troubled enough. But she wasn't aware of us anymore. She seemed to be staring at something that I couldn't see—dust motes or tiny aliens.

Pan's bedroom was like the rest of the house, high ceilings and natural wood moldings. There were no posters on his walls—paintings and drawings and photographs only. I would have taken more interest in the bookshelves and the dressing room and the private bathroom, but I was too rattled to be curious.

"Sorry about her," Pan said. "She keeps heading for death's door. But it's in a maze."

"What's actually wrong with her?" I asked. "Medically."

"No one knows. They diagnosed a bunch of things over the years, every disease you can think of. But the microbes must be afraid of her."

"So then what's this about me being a con artist?"

"She's always been kind of paranoid, distrustful, loopy. Now that's become most of who she is. My stepdad says she's daft, which I think is his polite way of ignoring her. Ever since I told her I was gay, she's been trying to find the right girl to cure me."

"This does wonders for my self-image, Pan. I really love that your grandmother thinks I'm not woman enough for her gay grandson."

"You're all the woman I need."

"You didn't tell her I shave my arms, did you? I've never told one of my girlfriends about that, not since fifth grade when I started. I'm trusting you with that information."

"She and I don't discuss your arms," he said. "We don't have that kind of relationship. Don't listen to her. You're beautiful. And trustworthy. I'll bet you haven't stolen anything since you stepped in this house."

"Give me time."

"I also believe she can sense heat, you know, like a missile? The more hurt you act, the better her aim."

"God," I said.

"Forget about her," he said, putting his hand on my face. "She thought I was here to read the gas meter the other day. Even if you went down and flashed your boobs, she won't remember it five minutes later."

"That would be a picture for your parents to walk in on," I said. "Me flashing your grandmother."

"Not at all. They'd be thrilled she finally made a friend. Anyway, she's already forgotten that she insulted you. And that you're here."

"I can't deal with this."

"I think you're beauteous and I'm all that matters," he said. "So, this is my room, but let's get something to eat before you go to work. I believe the fridge is full."

"I'm not going back down there," I said. "I'll take the window. I'll land in the snow."

"She's harmless. Look at my stepfather. She hasn't killed him yet, after all these years. And she's tried. Then again, he has the patience of a dead person."

"I'm not hungry."

"Yes, you are. Let's eat. You're not on a diet, are you?"

"Not today."

"Very good. Very, very good. Now come with me."

He took my hand and we went back down the stairs. We had to go right past his grandmother. She turned to us. I braced myself for another jagged observation.

"Is this your girlfriend?" she asked.

"We've been down that derelict road, Gram."

Suddenly she grabbed my arm and peered so intently that I thought she might hypnotize me.

"I don't care," she said, holding tight for such a frail woman, "I don't care if Jesus Christ himself comes down from heaven and tells me it's okay to be a homosexual. It will never be okay."

"I, uh, didn't know you were religious," I said, looking for a door. "I mean, your family isn't. And stuff."

"Don't be fresh with me, missy pants."

"Stop," Pan said.

"In my day, the nelly stayed at the organ bench where he couldn't do any harm. Now they want to march down the aisle in a wedding gown!"

I frowned. Pan would probably look better in a wedding dress than me.

"I think if he found the right girl," she continued.

Pan pried her hand off my arm. "Go toward the light, Gram. Faster."

"You look like a nice girl."

By now I didn't know who she was talking to. She looked so earnest that I almost forgave her for accusing me of planning to rob the place.

"Don't turn that TV on in here," she called as we walked toward the kitchen. "I can't stand the noise."

"You really are a good friend," Pan said, kissing my cheek.

"You're not kidding. Someday you'll appreciate me."

"Someday?" he asked with a smile so delicate I wanted to kiss him for real. But the afternoon had been confusing enough.

In the kitchen—which was so magnificent it could have been the set for a cooking show—we found his mom. In other circumstances I might first have noticed her lustrous hair and gorgeous skin. But what I really noticed was that she was holding a washrag and sniffing at cereal boxes. Pan's family had money, but so far they were definitely odd.

"What are you doing, Mother?" Pan asked.

"What does it look like I'm doing?"

"It looks like you're smelling the cereal. Then washing it."

"Exactly."

"Somewhere an airport dog is unemployed. This is my new friend Nia."

She turned and smiled. She was very beautiful, with high cheekbones and Pan's green eyes. But there was something aggressive in her look.

"Ah dah," she said. I was confused. Ah dah?

"Other people pronounce it Ada," Pan said, "but she has an aversion to long vowels. Second question, Mother. Why are you sniffing the cereal boxes?"

"For pesto."

"I believe we've heard enough."

"I had a jar of pesto in this." She held out a plastic grocery bag. "And it was leaking, and I'm afraid everything is going to smell like garlic for months"—she lowered her eyelids, raised an eyebrow—"if I put them in the cabinet without wiping them off first."

"Why are you whispering?" Pan asked her. "Still under surveillance?"

"Therefore each individual box needs to be wiped down."

"Why not put them in the dishwasher?"

"Here," she said, holding out a box with a sober design. She pulled it back, took a whiff, then wiped it. "It's been contaminated."

Pan looked at me. "There's really no explanation for my family, is there?"

I smiled. Ada was so confidently strange.

"All clean." She smelled the suspect package one final time before putting it into one of the long, windowed cabinets. She turned and saw that we were watching her. "Someday you'll both look back fondly on this moment," she said.

"We're going to eat something, Mother. But it's been really, really fun."

"Can't you wait until I get the fruits and vegetables washed? Ever heard of pesticides? Simply rinsing with water will not do. Soap is the key."

"Fight the good fight," said Pan, "but some other time. We have to get a snack. And you'd better go yell at Gram. She just accused Nia of stealing."

I swatted at him lightly. It was even worse in the repeating.

"I'm sorry, Nia," she said. "That really is obnoxious, but she tends to repeat things she's heard. My mother's illness makes her rather confused. And unpleasant."

"That's okay," I squeaked.

"No, it's not. I apologize for her now and for any future remarks. And there will be those."

"Gram's going to chase away my only friend here if you don't shut her up. Can't you get her a cat to fight with?"

"It's better here than Buckingham Heights, that hell of subdivisions and strip malls," she said. "Can I tell you something?"

"Please don't."

"If I'd had to hear one more time about Clarence's violin lessons in New York City with a *prominent* instructor—"

"Mother," Pan interrupted. "Retreat."

She looked annoyed, before the tiniest amusement peeked from her eyes.

"Have I gone on too long?"

"Rhetorical question." Pan took her arm and led her toward the dining room entrance.

"I'll talk to her," she said. "Fat lot of good it will do. Nice to meet you, Nia."

"Bye," I said. She left.

Pan motioned for me to sit at the table. Then he took a glass baking dish from the refrigerator, along with some cans. "Homemade chicken pot pie. Soda?"

"Any diet?"

"Not in this house. Though they're labeled as natural soda. Earth-based, I assume."

He poured us glasses of earth-based cola, then scooped big

plates of pie, nuked them for a minute or so, and placed one in front of me, along with a fork and a cloth napkin. "Mangia, signorina."

"I don't think you can use *mangia* with chicken pot pie."

Actually, it was better than what I usually got at home. His mom cooked basic food but with expensive ingredients. I didn't want to admit I could taste the difference, but it was true. Better ingredients, better food. Poverty was so unfair.

The back door opened, and a man walked in who I assumed was Pan's stepdad, Kevin.

"Hey, youngsters," he said with the smile of a kid holding a giant candy bar.

"Kev, this is Nia."

I stood up, and Kevin hugged me. "Nia, I'm so glad to meet you. We've heard nothing but good things."

"Thanks, Mr. Ashford," I said into his shoulder. When he let me go, he hugged Pan, who allowed it from his sitting position.

"Kevin," he said. He was so boyish-looking that the informality felt right. His thick, dirty-blond hair was combed tightly to one side like his mom had prepared him for a school photo. He wore goofy, round glasses on his pointy nose. He was what I would call nonthreatening, unaware handsome. I would have allowed myself to think he was even a little sexy if he weren't Pan's stepdad. Only in a few poses could you see that he was a grown-up, some crow's-feet, a bit tired when he wasn't smiling.

"Set up any interesting networks today?" Pan asked.

"Oh, I don't know how interesting it was," Kevin said. "You two having a snack?"

"Nia has to go to work, so I'm feeding her."

"That's a good boy. She works too hard. You work too hard, Nia, from what I hear."

"I don't have a job," Pan said, "my problems not being financial."

"Eat up," said Kevin. "No skipping meals in this house."

Kevin, I was to learn, loved to give advice, but it was never the finger-wagging-in-your-face that made you stop listening immediately. He also loved telling stories.

He put his hand on my shoulder. "Look at that boy," he said as if he and I were watching Pan from a distance. "Six feet tall. You know, Nia, James was not the kind of kid to climb on my lap, even when he was a little boy. And whenever he was taken away from his mom for any reason —any reason!—there was a hurricane of a tantrum."

"I could throw one now," Pan said.

"Aw, it wouldn't be the same," Kevin said.

"Mother and Gram have already sunk their fangs into Nia."

"Sorry. We are the fun family, after all."

"There's more food," Pan said. "Want some?"

"No. I don't want to spoil my supper. Can't eat like the old days."

"You might as well. We're having cereal for dinner. Freshly scrubbed."

"I won't ask," Kevin said. "You two have a good time. I mean it."

"I will," I said as he was leaving.

Then he turned and said to Pan, "Oh, and if you need me tomorrow, I am happy to go."

When he was gone, we chewed a few blissful moments. It was American food, as my mom would once have called it. She used to ignore any food without a red sauce whose name didn't end in a vowel. That was before Paolo. Since then, she rarely cooked the good stuff. Now all we had was cheap American food.

The flavors were making me love everything in the world. "Kevin's really nice, isn't he?" I said.

"Yeah, I guess. People always assume he's my real father, anyway."

"I would have if I hadn't known. The hair."

"His is getting gray. Although sometimes people mistake him for my older brother."

"I can see it."

"Which irritates Mother greatly."

"Your parents know you're ...."

"Oh, yeah. Long time ago."

"How did they take it?"

"I'm sure they always knew. I made my mother sew a Speedo for my GI Joe."

"That might have been a giveaway."

"Kevin had no problem with it. He said something like, 'You're still number one with us, buddy.' The kind of thing he would say."

"Oh my God, that's so sweet, Pan. Let's face it, the typical boy in this town won't even show his dad his report card."

"My mother was more concerned with how I was going to be treated at school, whichever one I was going to at the time."

"Did you? Have trouble?"

"There has been this and that. Some people think it's really cool, and they're kind of patronizing that way. Others can pretend that what they can't see doesn't exist."

"That's what I tried to do," I said. "But not for the same reasons."

"Will you ever forgive me?"

"If the food continues to stay of this quality."

"Kevin was good about it, but he doesn't know when to stop. He always wants to help, so he started on this gay slang thing, 'Let's go, girlfriend,' and crap that I would never say. I tried to give him the hint by fake laughing really loud, but he didn't take it. Finally, I had to punish him."

"Don't tell me. He's so good." At that moment I decided I would find out when Kevin's birthday was to make sure Pan didn't neglect it. I would do the same thing when Father's Day came around.

"It had to be done. This one time he was taking me for a haircut at a place called Ginger's Snap. Then he just had to say it was going to be our ladies' day at the beauty parlor."

"He was trying."

"Too hard. So I told him Ginger should shave his ass while he was there."

"That's awful."

"He thought so, too. He got this deep rose color in his face and spoke in an almost whisper, something like, 'You know I don't like it when you talk to me like that.'"

"Good. You deserved it."

"I was kind of scared of him then."

"Sounds innocent enough to me, Pan. Makes me like him even more."

"Yeah, he can come across like a dorky older brother, but he's a pretty good father all told. He went to all the tennis matches and school plays and orchestra concerts. Which is way more than I can say for my biological father."

What he meant was that he had contacted this biological father, whose name was Robertson, a while back, and the guy had responded. After months and months of hesitation and delays on both ends, they had finally arranged a meeting at a diner in New Rochelle, where Robertson lived. It didn't seem to me like the best setting for that kind of reunion.

"Are you nervous about seeing him?" I asked.

"I shouldn't be. I don't expect a lot from him. I just want to see for myself. He's the one who disappeared."

"That must be strange, meeting him for the first time—"

"I want you to come with me."

"That would be weird, right?"

"You should come. For moral support."

"What would I do while you're talking to him?"

"You could go to the Galleria. You can shop while you're waiting for me."

"And you know how I love to shop. Maybe the spring fashions will be in."

"Please? I'll buy you lunch. Give you the money for it anyway."

"I'd better not. It's my one Saturday off a month. I promised my mom I'd watch Paolo a few hours during the day."

"Pretty please? With chocolate pound cake on top?"

"Your mom made chocolate pound cake?" It was what he had served me and Amanda on our mutual birthday.

"And I know where it is."

"You know, Pan, any other boy would get a girl drunk so he could get her in bed."

"And your point?"

"That you, on the other hand, try to ply me with cake so I'll go on a road trip with you to see your dad."

"And?"

"And? And when is someone going to get me drunk and try to take advantage of me? When is it my turn to mean *no* when I say no?"

"I could take advantage of you now. With your approval, of course."

"You're a pansy."

"No one is totally, one hundred percent anything, Nia."

"I can't go. My mom needs me."

"Don't make me beg."

"I can't go in with you, right? You have to face him yourself. So what's the point?"

"You're my best friend. I want to talk to you as soon as it's over."

"You can call me as soon as it's over."

I finished my chicken pot pie, fighting the impulse to lick the plate.

"Cut me some cake," I said.

"No cake unless you agree."

"I'll look for it myself if you don't bring it to me." He got up and went to the counter and lifted the top of a cake saver. He cut me a moderate piece, put some vanilla ice cream on it, and placed it in front of me. Then he cut himself a giant one.

"Eat much?" I asked.

"I don't gain weight, either."

"Don't ever, ever say that to a girl," I said, then plowed in.

"So, is the answer still no?"

The cake was so good and Pan was so handsome, probably he could have gotten me to dance for his grandmother.

"Really, I would do it for you. But my mom looks forward to this one Saturday a month like it's parole. My baby brother has problems with his ears. Lots of screaming. It might be dangerous if she saw you taking me away after I'd stranded her."

"I could send her some cake."

"Nice try. But you stay home with a shrieking child all week long, then have your Saturday bowling taken away. Cake would not do it."

"I guess it's Kevin, then," he said, "though it will be strange talking to him about it. He'll only go so my mother won't have to. She tried to hide her bitterness, but it was like stuffing a hot air balloon into a lunch bag."

I was about to ask him why anyone had to go with him, why he couldn't just drive there by himself, but at that moment it struck me as cruel.

~

As it turned out, Robertson wasn't there when Pan and Kevin arrived, and he never showed up. After it was established by text that Robertson had forgotten and wanted to reschedule, they headed back home. Pan told me the basics on the phone and more of the details on Monday in school.

"Eh, who needs him?" he said with just the curl of a smile. We walked into the building without saying anything more. I couldn't imagine anyone not wanting to know his own son. I wanted to know Pan, even if he would never be mine in the way I had dreamed of. Good friend, not girlfriend. I could play it.

Chapter 5

Mungers Mills High School, according to Pan, was the opposite of Buckingham Heights, his last school, where the smartest kids ruled. The cool kids at MMHS were not particularly academic, and the smart kids suffocated under the social heap. I think there was some rule on the books about not allowing them on any sports team, because when the honor roll was published in the paper, I never saw any star player except Caspar Phillips.

I would not have been in the ruling class at Buckingham Heights. My grades were good, though I could have put in more effort, especially with the hard sciences, where I would get mostly Bs and an occasional A. I hadn't ever qualified for advanced math, and I probably wouldn't pursue any college credit courses when I was a senior. I found most high school classes pretty straightforward: Here was a task that wasn't simple, but you did it and you got rewarded. I couldn't understand why other kids got terrible grades. It was like never changing the oil in your car and letting it die.

The one exception was Science and Society, which might have been the most interesting class I'd ever taken. Mrs.

Mercado tried to "foster intelligent debate," as she put it. We saw pretty graphic videos and listened to guest speakers and watched demonstrations, and once a boy named James told us he was gay. I especially liked The Circle, where we tossed around our opinions on world health issues. I wasn't good at public speaking, so I didn't say much in The Circle, and Mrs. Mercado was a little sarcastic, which made me more nervous. But she did make me think, and I was caught up in every topic.

The problem with a democratic process was everyone had a right to express an opinion, including those who shouldn't, like Boz Samson. Amanda always referred to him as Samsonite because she said he was a piece of luggage that should be permanently lost at the airport. But hating Samsonite was as useless as hating a suitcase, which couldn't help being an empty, impervious shell.

I wanted The Circle to be something to show off to Pan, a strength in our school. But Samsonite always managed to lower expectations. He would say something ridiculous and then smile like he had just scored a touchdown, looking around the room for acknowledgment. One day, after some lively commentary from the usual participants like Amanda, Pan, and Sandy Willis, Samsonite started to argue about health care. But he went on so long and in so many circles that it was hard to tell what he was arguing for or against. He seemed to be holding people accountable for getting sick, as if they did it deliberately.

Pan interrupted his drone. "People would live longer if they could all get to doctors, surgeons. If they could get their medications."

Samsonite sneered something under his breath.

"What's that, Boz?" Mrs. Mercado asked, with a hint of sharpness.

"Nothing."

"You sure?"

All expression left his face.

She waited in the way teachers do that makes five seconds seem like the Bronze Age.

Caspar Phillips broke the tension with his voice that was so bass it could have been electronically altered: "There are no simple solutions to complex problems." He appeared to be addressing Boz. "If diseases were simple, we would have wiped them all out a long time ago. You can't blame people for contracting them."

Caspar was a curious person. He had started in our school as a sophomore. He was a big, hulking guy, a talented football player, but there was an old man inside him. The rhythm of his speech was one thing. When you first heard him, you were sure he was doing an impression. Then when you realized he wasn't, you wouldn't be listening to what he was saying, because how he talked was so interesting. When you got beyond that peculiar voice, you saw that he chose his words deliberately.

"Boz? Your response?" Mrs. Mercado said, with the tiniest eyebrow lift.

But Caspar answered instead. "My dad told me there had been talk in the past of concentration camps for people with certain infections. Putting everyone with contagious diseases on an island somewhere so they wouldn't spread them. That sounds like a pretty dangerous precedent."

"Precedent," Samsonite repeated, as if he were learning a word in another language.

Caspar turned to Samsonite, though his face remained nearly immobile. "Setting the standard."

"I know, dude," said Samsonite. Probably he didn't, but maybe he would shut up.

"If they put them on an island, they couldn't spread their disease." This was from Patrick Torno, Samsonite's best friend, who rarely talked. But his silence was as menacing as the few words he ever said. He slouched in his desk, legs extended, cap pulled down over the tops of his eyelids. Since Pan's revelation, Torno could barely look at him, and when he did, it was with unblinking disgust.

Caspar continued. "If you start banishing people, how do you know where to stop? I don't think we want to be like that." He cleared his throat. He was definitely interesting and smart, even if listening to him was a commitment.

"Yeah," said Torno. He gave Caspar a quick, upward nod, as if dismissing him.

The bell rang and the discussion was over. As Pan and I stepped into the hall, Patrick Torno gave him a furtive slap upside the head. It was incongruous because Pan was tall, and tall people generally didn't get slapped in the head by shorter people.

Except from the initial flinch, Pan didn't react. I pulled him the other way.

"You need to tell Guten about that," I said, meaning the vice principal.

"Don't let it bother you," he said. "No point in giving them attention during their de-evolution." Pan was so nonchalant I was beginning to wonder if the slap had actually happened.

From behind us we heard Caspar's slow voice: "You shouldn't let them get away with that."

We both spun around.

"Sorry," he said. "I overheard you." Then he kept going, as if he hadn't been speaking to us.

We looked at each other, thrown off.

"Is he like the school visionary or something?" Pan asked.

"I don't know," I said. But I was now more curious about

him than ever.

Chapter 6

It was time for Pan to meet my family. At least to meet Mom and Paolo. I had avoided bringing him over as long as I could, hesitating and fumbling when he insisted. I told him the truth, sort of, that I liked being away from my house and all the responsibilities I had there. I told him it was a pleasant escape for me in his big, fancy old place. He had a TV in his room, so we could watch terrible shows and make fun of them. And his house was in a nice part of town. Kids on my street called it the rich neighborhood because that's where the doctors and lawyers had always lived. But he insisted I take him to my side of the tracks, and eventually got suspicious of my stalling.

"Why are you keeping me away?" he asked. "Is it the G thing? I understand if it is."

"No, not at all," I said. "I never even thought of that. In fact, I told my mom, and she was fine with it, like I knew she would be." I didn't tell him of Dad's stony reaction.

"So?"

So the whole truth was I was embarrassed to have Pan at my never-quite-clean house, with the constant howl of a baby brother. I didn't want him to see the neighborhood I lived in. And worst, I was ashamed of the way Mom looked these days. She had given up on her appearance since Paolo was born. Everything she wore made her look older than she was— cheap polyester pants and T-shirts with loud designs. She still had beautiful hair, thick and black, but it had streaks of gray that she could easily have colored. Instead, as if to make it clear she was in retreat, she covered her hair entirely with a skull-design cotton bandana.

But he didn't care, so one day after school we walked toward my place instead of his. I was so anxious that I blurted, "My house doesn't smell good. I might as well warn you."

"Don't worry."

"It's not offensively bad, like farts or cat pee. It's just kind of stale. Old, musty house odor. No amount of cleaning will scare it out."

"My grandmother keeps our house at ninety degrees all year long. How good can it smell?"

"Look, Pan, my dad's auto shop failed, and he's still paying off the business loan. Now he repairs cars for someone else. And my mom is unemployed. We don't live in a castle."

"You're being melodramatic."

"You'll see."

My heart went cold when Mom met us in the living room wearing her usual ensemble.

"This is my friend Pan."

"Pan?" she asked. "I thought you said it was James."

"Long story," I said.

"Nice to meet you. I'm JoAnne." They shook hands.

"You must be Nia's sister," Pan said. "Is your mom home?"

Mom's smile started in her eyes, and she suddenly looked younger than she had in years. "Just for that," she said, "I'm fixing you a snack. Sit. Relax." She scuttled out of the room with a new energy.

Before long we smelled garlic sautéing.

"Come on in here," she called. On the table were two bowls of pasta. "Just a little spaghetti to take the edge off."

"This is incredible," Pan said, twirling a huge circle onto his fork and sticking it in his mouth. "You just whipped this up? Will you be my mom, too?"

Mom's eyes were dancing. And I realized that she had at some point removed the bandana and tied up her hair.

"It's just garlic and oil," she said. "Nothing to it." She didn't eat with us, but she was full of questions. "So, Mr. Pan, are you starting to look for colleges? Do you know what you want to be when you grow up?"

"Well, my stepfather does computers and my mother was a psychologist. So neither of those."

"What do you mean she was?" I asked, though I was more interested in Mom's return to cooking.

"She doesn't practice anymore. Maybe I'll be a doctor. Lawyer. A few years ago I thought about professional tennis, but now we're here, so that's not going to happen. Nia says she's going with me, wherever I go."

"Not likely," I said. "The community college looks good enough."

"With her grades she could probably get a scholarship," Mom said, "unlike her mom and dad, who were not so swift in their day. All my kids are going to get four-year degrees, if I have to do their work for them."

"Two years at Mohegan CC ought to give me some career inspiration," I said. "It would be nice to get a job around here, close to my family. Teaching maybe."

"Teaching must be the last industry left in Mungers Mills," Pan said, then worked another spool of spaghetti into his mouth.

"Teachers can spend the summers with their kids," I said. "That's all I really want—a real job, a family."

"A few years ago I would have nixed Mohegan for Nia," Mom said. "Her brother Teo is at the University at Holland Park, in the business school. No small accomplishment. But with Paolo in the picture, I could use a couple more years of help. Then she will be transferring, no question. Her dad and I got married a few weeks out of high school." She breathed in deep at the memory. "I'm boring you kids."

"Not at all," said Pan, "although I was thinking about bringing you home to cook for us. Keep going. I like hearing people's origin stories."

"Well," she continued, "Tony and I thought we were so happy about no more classes, no more 'in' groups. We thought we were tasting freedom. Who'd have known it would leave such an aftertaste?"

"What do you mean, Mom?" Pan asked. I looked at him. His eyes were set on her, very interested. And he didn't call his own mom *Mom.*

"Oh," she nearly sang, "instead of taking the advice of our elders and going to school, we took jobs and made money and had babies. Now, I don't regret my children, but after fifteen years of sitting in an office, I decided I wanted more from life than working for a doctor. I wanted that piece of paper. Then I got pregnant again. It was during my first semester at Mohegan."

"No cause for celebration?" he asked.

"Little Paolo has ... his ears have been a problem, and they make him, let's say, cranky." Mom and I exchanged a look. *Cranky* was generous.

"I tried to take a course or two but couldn't keep up," she continued. "Nia helped me through it all. She practically adopted her little brother, but I had to give up. College became a disappointment instead of a dream. That's why I tell my kids, 'Go to school. Get an education. You can always have a family.'"

At that moment Paolo wailed from his crib, loud and angry.

"Or not." She started to get up.

"Mom, no," I said, "I'll get him." We were done eating, anyway. Pan got up, too.

"When we come back," he said, "I want to hear about you managing the doctor's office. My mother used to have her own practice, and she said the office manager was the most important person there."

"Oh!" Mom said. I couldn't remember the last time I'd seen her delighted.

~

Waking up was just one of the many things that Paolo resented. His wake-up cry was more like despair. Usually, when he saw me, he started to cry harder, as if to convince me he hadn't been faking. He did turn up the volume, for a second, but then he saw Pan and he was startled silent. Pan picked him up before I could warn him, but instead of shouting an objection, Paolo took an interest in this new being, especially the wavy, blond hair.

I got out my phone and took a picture. Paolo never liked strangers—or anybody—and he never got quiet this fast. Paolo giggled as Pan nuzzled and tickled him, then played peekaboo. It was like magic.

"I should call my mom up here," I said. "To witness."

"What are you talking about?" Pan asked. "He's a cute little kid." He held Paolo up and made him laugh again. I looked at the baby with wonderment. Laughing. Life was full of possibilities.

Pan carried Paolo downstairs.

"I almost called an ambulance," Mom said, amazed, "when he stopped crying like that. Paolo's first friend."

"Does this mean my brother's gay, too?" I asked.

Mom grunted and said, "No one will ever use that word to describe this child."

As we walked to the pharmacy I told Pan about Paolo, about his ears and his noise. He was otherwise a normal baby, just not a happy one. Each insult and every burden in Paolo's life made me want to shield him from the next.

"No one ever tells us he's cute, or anything like the compliments most babies get," I said. "They say he's big. This old woman peeked into his stroller once and I swear she looked disappointed. And she said, 'Now that's a baby.'"

Pan frowned, almost a grimace, but didn't say anything.

"After Mrs. Burrell explained fago to us, I was pretty sure that's what I felt for my baby brother."

"Fago?"

I told him about it.

"I love Paolo," I said. "Of course I do—but I'm also a little bit afraid for him."

"Afraid how?" Pan asked.

"That he'll start to sense Mom and Dad's disinterest. That he won't have any friends. No girlfriend. That one kid in school no one wants to be."

"It's way premature, worries like that," said Pan. "And you're taking the best care of him you can."

We walked a while.

"I like the smell of your house," Pan said, finally. "Garlic and basil. It makes me feel comfy."

Chapter 7

I suppose it had something to do with my modest ambition, but I really liked my job. Maybe I should have had some fago for Polaski's Pharmacy, because it was one of the few long-standing businesses left on the main strip of downtown Mungers Mills, and it tried to survive against the two chain drugstores on the outside of town.

Pan once said that the old buildings could be a movie set for a period piece. Sometimes I imagined them in their prime, imposing brick and steel, fancy concrete moldings, cornerstones with dates like 1875. I tried to picture a time when downtown was proud and necessary, the sidewalks and streets bustling with people and trolleys. Now it was begging. Our store was hardly a gem, old and forlorn underneath abandoned offices upstairs. The Historic Preservation Board kept the buildings from being torn down, but that meant they stayed up, often empty.

Pan's parents made a special point of coming down to support an independent business, and therefore my continued employment. The store owner stopped in once in a while to whine about sales. We were always barely holding on. Most of our customers were elderly, or very poor, or living in the residences for people with developmental disabilities nearby, and they came in only for little things.

I'd worked there since I'd turned sixteen, actually a little before, and now I worked more hours. My parents hadn't forced me to find a job, and I knew Mom would rather have me help more with Paolo. But if I didn't work, I would have to ask them for spending money, which I dreaded.

I got such a silly glow of contentment from working on a Friday night. Pan would usually spend half a shift with me, talking, helping out, walking casually to the door when the owner came in. There were insurance concerns, and since he was not an employee, he was not supposed to be there lifting boxes. It wasn't an exciting life trying to camouflage my non-boyfriend's presence while we stacked deodorant and body wash. Other kids my age were at parties. Yet I often felt completely fine in our decaying part of town with my predictable job. Since Mom was making me go to college, a career as a pharmacy clerk was not an option. She had warned me that someday the coziness and predictability would not be a consolation when I looked back at my wasted youth. But I wasn't feeling the dissatisfaction yet.

The job was not all that difficult. Sometimes I could do some reading while I waited for customers to straggle in. My only concern, besides whether the pharmacy would survive another year, was the assistant manager, Tammie Speers. Tammie had to be reckoned with when our shifts collided, especially if I had homework to do, because she had this work ethic that any sitting around—on my part, not hers—was a waste of company money.

Tammie had also taken to flirting with Pan. I understood the reason—I'd done it too—but she was worse. It had crossed my mind to clarify for her why this was pointless, but I'm sure Tammie would just pretend she already knew and then lecture me about acceptance. At least when he was around she was on her best behavior, like she was with the pharmacist or the owner, and not bossing me. Pan was his most complimentary with her, and she loved it.

Tammie was twenty-eight, with no long-term relationship in sight. That didn't matter to me, except she was clearly obsessed with finding one. When she had as much as a date, the words 'my boyfriend' found their way into every other sentence. When that relationship crashed, so did the references. Until the next guy. One boyfriend in the series had even risen to fiancé status before she stopped mentioning him altogether and stopped flashing the ring.

My mom used Tammie in her life lessons many times. "She's a perfect example of what happens when you don't go to college and make something of yourself. More perfect than me."

I knew I was never going to like Tammie, though I tried to have some sympathy. She didn't make it easy. Besides always looking to keep me busy, she wasn't the most competent employee, or even that hard a worker. She didn't have patience for the kind of menial tasks she assigned to me. She did a lot of flitting around, sounding important. When she talked to a customer, she got very loud and formal.

"Now here is your receipt, which I can hand to you or put in your bag, whatever you wish. I can also send an email receipt. Please keep the receipt in case you need to make a return, and please have a very good evening."

Despite the formality, she was not good with customers. When there was something I couldn't figure out on the register or a customer who complained and wouldn't go away, Tammie would buzz around for a few seconds, bark some pointless comments, then disappear. I'd wind up handling the problem myself, at which point she would be back, asking how it had worked out, then explaining how I could have done it better. She would sprinkle in phrases like "When I worked the front desk, before I was assistant manager .... " When I'd first gotten the job, I would get defensive and say I'd done the best I could. She'd smile the placating smile an older person gives a kid, and tell me it was all a learning experience. When I eventually figured her out, I stopped defending myself. Her life made me uneasy. I knew what it was like to want a boyfriend and not have one. And I wondered, if I didn't go to college, would I be the same way someday, annoying a younger employee because I could? That was as good a reason to get an education as any.

One night Pan was studying for a test and couldn't come down to play at the pharmacy until later. A sleigh-riding scene blinked in our window, forcing cheeriness onto Broad Street. I was doing some reading. Tammie and I were alone in the store most of the evening. A sweet, older customer named Larry walked in shortly before closing time. He was looking for a birthday card for the woman who cooked at his residence. Much to his misfortune, Tammie was hovering near the rack.

"Hi, Larry," she shouted, even though he was not hearing impaired. "You have to hurry because we're going to close soon. Hurry."

He looked worried. I would have gladly stayed open a little longer to let him finish because he was painstaking and serious about his meager purchases.

"Do you want a funny card?" Tammie barked. "Do you want one like this?" Then she practically screamed, "Funny?"

I'm sure Larry knew what *funny* meant.

"Do you want one that's got a picture on the front? Picture? Or do you like these cartoon ones, Larry? You have to hurry, Larry, we're closing. We open at nine and we close at nine. You know that by now." She continued plucking more cards for him, getting in his face like a lip-reader while he got more and more frustrated and began counting the change from his pocket. I watched in agony.

"The rules apply to everyone," she sang.

"I've got it, Tammie," I said.

"What?"

"I've got it. It's okay."

"If customers stay late, we have to stay late," she said. "*I* have to stay late."

"I know. I'll take this, and I'll balance and close up after."

Then Pan walked in.

"Tammie, hi," he said. "Wow, have you lost weight or what? I mean, you were never heavy, but now you're downright lean."

"Finally someone noticed!" Tammie said, forgetting Larry and switching to flirtation mode. I stole the chance to let Larry choose a card and pay for it with change that he counted out again and again. By the time Tammie returned to earth, Larry was on his way out the door with a slim white bag. Tammie called a goodbye to him and waved energetically, then said, "And remember, we close at nine, sir."

I did my end-of-shift routines. When Pan and I were about to leave, Tammie said, "James, Nia seems so uptight lately. Maybe you can bring a smile to her face. You both have a great night. Bye bye, kids."

I could barely talk as we walked home.

"Something wrong?" he asked.

"She is so miserable sometimes," I said. "You got the tail end of the Larry drama."

"The way she kept shouting his name when I first walked

in, I thought someone named Larry was in a coma."

"Poor guy. I had to put some money in for him. I couldn't let him keep counting his coins, so I just took what he had and told him it was perfect. Not exactly honest."

"At least you got him out of there."

"Yeah. She once told me 'those people' will never learn if you do things for them. The whole point is to get them to be independent."

"Like her."

"She thinks she taught him a lesson, but what she really taught him was to be afraid of coming into our store."

"Forget it. Soon enough she'll mess with the wrong person, and she'll be history."

Something about that depressed me—Tammie losing such a humble job.

"She's not qualified for much else," I said.

"She does have managerial experience," he said.

"Assistant," I said. "Assistant managerial."

Chapter 8

In early February, Pan and I had to take Paolo to an interview at a daycare center. Mom was meeting with a counselor at Mohegan yet again, this time to investigate the nontraditional student route, and she would need two days a week off to take a couple classes and do the homework. I had offered her some of the money I'd earned at the pharmacy to help out.

"The dream may not be completely dead," she said. As it turned out, the day care required an interview, and the only time the woman could do it was at the same time as Mom's college appointment.

Since I'd never gone to day care as a child, I was surprised that Paolo, at age one, had to audition for a spot. I was not optimistic.

When the day came, Pan pulled up in his mom's car. My mom leaned in toward his open window as I got Paolo in his seat in the back.

"Make sure you two do all the talking," she said. "Keep him quiet. Let them think he's the most silent baby on the planet."

"We'll try, Mom," Pan said.

"James, you may have to come with me every time I drop him off."

"Sure. We'll open the door, hand him off, and run like we're on fire."

"Fine. Afterward I'll cook something nice for you." She blew a kiss to us.

Paolo, who had been unhappy about having to wear his snowsuit, was even more displeased that Pan was sitting in the front seat. Since a car is only so big and can hold in quite a bit of sound, I had to drive his mom's car, which added to the anxiety. Pan had to sit in the back next to him, bent sideways so Paolo could pull his hair.

A few minutes' drive from the center of town where I lived and we were practically in the country. The homes were farther apart, huge yards and long driveways, no sidewalks, lots of evergreens and bushes. The better-off people were moving there, out of the city, even out of the nice neighborhood Pan lived in. The day care had green shutters and trim. A painted sign on the lawn said Green Goose Day School.

The owner introduced herself as Mrs. Purcell and led us into her office. We could hear children playing in another part of the house. She was a short penguin of a woman. I quickly took Paolo's snowsuit off so he wouldn't get hot and start yelling. Then Pan took him. Mrs. Purcell was pleasant enough. That is, until she got right into Paolo's face. "What a little chunk he is!"

Paolo let out a scream. Pan laughed, turned Paolo toward him. Paolo relaxed and grabbed some of Pan's hair.

"Doing his vocal warmups," Pan said. "I predict he's a tenor."

"He likes you," I said to Mrs. Purcell, which was really

dumb.

Pan stayed busy trying to keep Paolo from destroying my mom's future while Mrs. Purcell asked me a lot of what I thought were very personal questions about my family—how many of us and how old, what jobs we had, and if anyone had ever been convicted of a crime. Finally, after she'd asked for way too much information, she closed her notebook and looked over at Pan and Paolo.

"He's good with kids," she said. "He'll make a good dad someday." My heart beat a couple aches that Pan would never be a dad to a child of mine.

"Yeah," I said, "Paolo adores him."

"Your boyfriend, I assume."

I knew any hint of truth might destroy Paolo's chances. You could never tell with old people which side of this fence they were on.

"Yeah, my boyfriend." I looked at him. She had really given me a compliment.

"Are we ready to go, babe?" Pan said in his James Bond-iest voice.

For a second I drank in the rapture of that. "Sure, uh, hon."

"Let me hold that chunk of a baby," Mrs. Purcell said, standing up and holding out her hands.

Pan looked unsure. I was struck motionless.

"Here we go, baby boy," Pan said, handing Paolo to Mrs. Purcell, but backing him away so that Paolo was still facing him, thinking it was a game. Paolo, with a drooly grin, gurgled a laugh. Pan kept mugging as he let go, and Paolo was unaware that he'd been passed off.

"Adorable," Mrs. Purcell said. Paolo whipped his head around and saw that he'd been taken captive. There was a second of silence—Pan and I had stopped breathing—as Paolo took in the full horror of Mrs. Purcell. She turned him, put her head against his, cooing.

At that moment Paolo emitted a guttural noise explosion. We were used to them, but Mrs. Purcell was startled.

"That's okay, sweet cheeks," she said, nuzzling his face and stomach. Paolo stopped for a second, terror and indignation fighting for control of his pudgy little face. His next wail was louder, if that was possible.

"Now, now," she said, sounding a bit annoyed. "Would you like to try the indoor swing? It's too cold to go outside this time of year. We'd have to get you all bundled up."

Paolo stopped again, as if not believing her impertinence. Then he erupted, like a maniacal sound-effects machine. Pan tried to be nonchalant as he lifted our little ball of fury from Mrs. Purcell and turned him. Paolo saw Pan and stopped immediately.

"That's interesting," Mrs. Purcell said, more scornful than interested. "I usually have a way with fussy children. Let's try again." Before I could object, she took Paolo. Pan looked like she had pulled off his arm. Paolo, having had quite enough, vomited this time, and like dragon fire. She yelped and practically tossed him to me.

"He's had a little tummy ache," I said. "Really, I'm so sorry. His teeth give him a lot of trouble, too."

She picked up a diaper and began wiping the mess off herself.

Paolo had by now forgotten his nightmare and was laughing at Pan, who had taken him from me and was putting the snowsuit back on him. We were all tainted by his barf, though Mrs. Purcell had gotten the worst of it.

"I'll need to call your mother," she said. "We need to discuss his separation anxiety. And I hope he doesn't have the flu."

"No," I said. "I don't think so."

"Of course I can't believe you'd bring a child with the flu out in public."

I couldn't think of anything but apologies. I considered throwing myself at her little penguin feet, begging her not to reject him, promising we would find a baby-size muzzle. "I'm so sorry," I said, but Pan interrupted.

"He doesn't have the flu," he said, looking Mrs. Purcell in the eye. "He's just anxious. As babies are."

Mrs. Purcell seemed to catch something in his tone.

"Thanks for stopping by," she said, and moved toward the door. Pan carried my oblivious brother.

"Bye," I said. I could hear the pleading in my voice when I added, "I think he'll like it here. It's perfect. Lots of space."

"We'll see."

"It's a day care," Pan said. "Kids cry. He'll fit right in."

"Have a nice day," she said, guiding us out.

We were solemn in the car after. Finally, Pan said, "Well, she was a flaming amateur."

I agreed but didn't have the energy to say so.

"I'll be glad to babysit twice a week. Especially since I evidently insulted Hagatha and nailed the coffin shut. I'll even skip school if Mama Fazzino needs me."

"Thanks, but I'm afraid Paolo's going straight into foster care when she hears about this."

We pulled up in front of my house.

"Good," I said. "She's not home yet."

"Yeah. I'm not sure I could stand the look on her face."

Chapter 9

Mrs. Burrell, in English, was our most intense teacher. Every movement was charged, like she was dancing on electricity. She reminded me of a Chihuahua, a smart, interested, determined Chihuahua. There wasn't a single worksheet that she wasn't excited and exacting about. Now she was having us take a real life experience and making things up so it sounded more like a story. We spent a lot of time reading famous short stories and figuring out what elements made them work. We used real people's journals and diaries to get ideas.

"Uh, how long is this supposed to be?" Samsonite had asked.

"The story can be as long or as short as you want, but it has to have a complete story arc," Mrs. Burrell responded. Unlike Mrs. Mercado, she wasn't too concerned with a free flow of conversation with people like him. So when he attempted to ask another question, she reviewed what a story arc was in details that I'm sure he ignored.

"I'm going to copy each piece for workshopping, as it's called. You're going to give your opinions on the story to the person who wrote it, both in discussion and on paper. You will be graded not only on your story—please listen to this carefully—but also on how well you participate in each workshop. Your responses will have to follow specific guidelines which we'll develop together."

Samsonite raised his hand. Instead of answering, Mrs. Burrell proceeded to generate guidelines with us. I started to see that this was going to be as hard as a science lab, and I wouldn't be able to get by with regular effort this time.

When I tried to write a draft, my creative process dried up so fast it was dripping dust. I didn't think my story was especially good, though I had Pan and Mom read it before I handed it in, and they liked it much better than I did.

The workshop schedule listed me near the beginning, and I was brittle tense that day. I was tempted to skip school and claim I had a dentist's appointment, but Mrs. Burrell would reschedule me, which would only prolong the agony. Pan said he would defend me, and I also figured out a good strategy for being in the spotlight, which was taking profuse notes while my story was being discussed. I wanted something to do with my hands while my story was being judged, rather than fighting to look calm.

But there was no brutality. The class wasn't exactly enthralled by my story about a college kid who makes his bunk bed collapse on his roommate. I had gotten the idea from my older brother, Teo, who, as a freshman at UHP, had been in a dorm room with two other guys who hated each other. I might have thrown in a little of "The Tell-Tale Heart" or "The Lottery." Most of the comments were about the incompleteness of the story, and how the bed collapsing needed to be more important than just a premise. That made sense and gave me some new ideas.

Pan did defend me, and without sounding defensive. "I like

that evil-in-the-hearts-of-men concept," he said in his smooth tone. "We get to see into the head of someone whose anger has taken over. It shows the irrationality from the inside."

"Yes," said Mrs. Burrell, "and she also has a nice way with figures of speech."

That was kind, but mostly I wanted it to be over. Once the focus had passed from me, workshopping was kind of fun. I enjoyed it more with each class. I didn't say anything out loud, but I liked writing the critiques and listening to the discussions. Using a new set of words to respond to the stories made me feel more like an adult. And Mrs. Burrell was taking us very seriously, like she cared what we thought.

I knew Pan's would be excellent, since everything he did was. But when he gave me a draft, I had to read it a second time to understand why I didn't like it.

"This is a slam on Samsonite and Patrick Torno," I said. "That's all it is."

"Yeah?"

"I know what she's going to say. She's going to say it's not a real story because it's not truthful."

"It is truthful. They're idiots. Twin idiots."

"You have Samsonite falling in love with the school groundskeeper?"

"It could happen."

"Who bears a striking resemblance to Patrick Torno?"

"So?"

"So the ending is a joke. I can't believe you have them sailing off together on a riding mower."

"I thought you'd think it was funny, Nia."

"It's hilarious, it really is. Let's keep it for a joke between us. But don't go public with it."

"Well ...."

"Besides, I'm afraid of Patrick Torno. I'm afraid of what's going on in his head."

"Not much."

"So why give him the honor of a starring role in your story?"

"If you insist, I'll write something new."

He did, and this time it was elegant. He wrote about a boy who meets his real dad and manages to help the guy stop drinking. It made me choke up a little, and the class gave him good reviews, with some raves. Torno and Samsonite didn't say a word, just a few snickers and sneers.

Eventually we read Samsonite's story. There were no limits on subject matter, which turned out to be a problem. I don't know why Mrs. Burrell didn't make him rewrite it before his turn on the hot seat, because parts of it were incomprehensible. But I knew it was directed at Pan. A man pretends to be gay so he can have an affair with his very heavy female secretary. Every time the boss had to say a word with an *s* in it, Samsonite replaced it with *th* for lisping. The boss made constant references to anal and oral sex. At the end the boss revealed himself as straight after all, and he ran away with his girlfriend, who tore off her fat suit to reveal a stunning body. In other words, it made no sense.

We got the copies on Thursday and were supposed to have read it and written notes for Friday's class. That's what I was doing when Pan came in to the pharmacy that night.

"Why waste your energy on a fool?" he asked. "If she gives him even a D on it, we'll know she's the one wearing the fat suit."

My stomach turned a notch. If people liked anything about it, were amused by or praised any part of it, I would have to admit that our school was hopeless.

The next day in class Pan sat frozen like the Sphinx. The kids who did speak up—I didn't—were usually careful with Mrs. Burrell's guidelines. Not this time. Most of the comments were so hostile that within a few minutes Samsonite's satisfied grin became a tremble.

"I didn't believe any of it. It was like you made us read seven pages to get to a punch line," Amanda said, breaking the ice for what became a flow of reproach. "You're not taking your story seriously. Who are these people?"

"It's a long joke," said Sandy Willis. "Not a very good one, either. I was waiting for something to make sense. It never did."

Caspar Phillips was the one person in the class I expected some diplomacy from. His comments were gentler than the rest, but not by much. "I couldn't figure out the point of the story. Why does the guy pretend to be gay in order to have an affair with his secretary? If she had a husband, then maybe I could see it, if the husband worked in the same office. Which he doesn't."

"Yeah," Amanda said. "Did the boss just start acting like a flamethrower when they began the affair? Wouldn't the other people in the office wonder about that?"

"And no one in the office minded him talking about getting it up the butt constantly?" Sandy Willis asked. The class laughed at that—most of the class, anyway.

"Didn't anyone notice that the secretary suddenly got fat?" Amy Conrad asked in her pinched voice.

"I felt like I was wasting my time reading it," said Sandy. "I could see if you were being ironic, criticizing fat shaming. But it's not."

Amanda brought it home: "I had to look it up, but the word is spelled *f-a-g-g-o-t*, not *f-a-g-e-t*."

"Maybe it's French," said Caspar, making everyone laugh

again, though he didn't look as if he'd intended to. Samsonite appeared to be shrinking in his seat.

There was only one positive remark, and it wasn't from the teacher. Probably even Mrs. Burrell couldn't find anything redeeming. Instead, it came from Patrick Torno. "I thought the surprise ending was pretty cool. I wasn't expecting it."

"I was surprised that I made it to the end," Pan said.

Torno looked like he was about to draw a gun.

"I made it to the end," said Caspar Phillips, like a tape playing too slowly , "because I wanted to see if there was a payoff. But I drew the conclusion that you were making fun of writing a story."

Mrs. Burrell usually interrupted people who veered from the guidelines, which everyone had. Instead, she stayed quiet while one person after another shredded the story. Finally, she broke in.

"Maybe we need to review notes about plot lines and character development," she said, and then took specifics from Samsonite's story as examples of what not to do. There was no mistaking how sharp she was being, but she did try to offer suggestions for him to rewrite by including an occasional, "What you could do here, Boz, is ...."

I wondered if she had meant to let Samsonite hang himself by not stopping him from using this crappy draft for the critique. As cruel as he had intended to be, the whole episode had been a disaster for him.

But someone had to pay. After school Pan was packing up at his locker and I was waiting for him. While he was bent over getting books, Samsonite and Patrick Torno appeared, and Samsonite slammed him from behind. Pan's head practically got caught inside. Torno gave one more shove before I fully grasped the situation and shrieked something at them.

Samsonite was down the hall already, but Torno was not in a rush. I turned back to Pan, afraid of what I might see. He had straightened himself, blood on his lip, a whitish scrape down his face.

"Are you okay?"

He blotted the blood from his lip with the back of his hand and examined it.

"I'm going to tell Mrs. Guten now," I said, louder than I needed to be for someone right next to me. "This is a bunch of crap." I had never been in a room alone with our vice principal, and I was a little afraid of her, but I was moving on furious energy.

"No. What's she going to do? Suspend them? For no brain folds?"

"It's harassment. It's illegal. You can get thrown out of school for smoking a cigarette. They've got to care about people getting their heads smashed in."

"Is it smashed in? If they destroyed my face, they're dead."

"I'm going. She's hearing it from me."

Pan licked at his lip.

"Salt. Maybe a little Coke, too."

"Does it hurt?"

"Only in my heart."

"Pan, let's go to the nurse, and then I'm going to see Guten and tell her what's going on before they do something really obnoxious."

It was only minutes later that Pan and I were walking to his house, incident not reported.

"Why am I letting you get away with this?" I asked.

"What?"

"They beat you up and I'm the one fighting with you to turn them in."

"That's one of your many qualities. Always looking out for your man."

"You won't let me look out for my man."

"Think about it. If we tell, they'll say I hit on one of them or something like that. Perfect justification for kicking the gay boy's ass. The rich gay boy."

"But what if you do nothing? Just let this go on forever?"

"They don't have that kind of perseverance. And wasn't it worth a little head bashing to watch Samsonite swinging in the wind today?"

"No. Nothing's worth it."

"Did you see his face? He has this sparkle, like a stand-up comedian who just knows he's going to kill. And then one person starts on him, then the next, and before you know it, he looks like his IQ went viral. All his fans abandoned him. And I didn't pay a single one of them."

"Well, I'm glad Mungers Mills proved its integrity today. But I am going to report this if you don't."

"Don't push me into a corner, Nia. I've already been in a locker."

We walked awhile. His indifference confounded me, but there was no penetrating it.

"You're not going to cooperate with me, are you? I really think you need to tell someone—Kevin at least— about those two."

"I'll be all right. Just always promise to be my friend. That's all."

"Come on."

"Promise?"

I didn't answer.

"Nia? Are you still there?"

"Yeah."

"Yeah you're still there, or yeah you'll be my friend

forever?"

"Both. I'm sulking."

"One of the many reasons I loves ya so much. Now promise."

"Okay, I promise," I said, looking at him. "If someone better doesn't come along."

But he didn't smile. He just gave me this small lift of his eyes, where I could see beyond his self-assurance.

Chapter 10

Before the bell, Mrs. Burrell had passed out Caspar's story for us to review over the weekend. Caspar was also on my mind because that morning Dr. Jackson had announced his birthday, and during lunch Samsonite and his table of friends had made a huge deal of it, singing and shouting. Caspar had looked miserable.

At work that night I read the story, and I was really gripped by it. I wanted to read it again. Then I heard Tammie broadcasting at an unnecessary decibel.

"Angela, you have to go to the bathroom before you leave your house. You can't come in here every time and use ours."

Angela was maybe fifty. From enough of a distance, you might think she was somebody's grandmother. Up close you could see that she was frail and jittery. She always came in to buy gum, which meant she was in fact a paying customer. But the price of gum didn't include bathroom privileges, according to Tammie.

The argument went on a few minutes, back and forth, Tammie's piercing volume resonating through the store, dwarfing Angela's muffled responses. I considered locking my register and going back to plead Angela's case, but before I could decide, she shuffled out the front without buying so much as a gumball.

Tammie came to the register.

"Those residents!" she said. "I'm going to call her house and tell the folks on duty that they have to make sure the clients use the potty before they go out."

I said nothing. She waited, then turned and marched back to whatever she had pretended to be doing before. I went back to Caspar's story.

It was about a high school senior whose only wish for a graduation present was that his older brothers would show up at the commencement. They were his dad's kids from a previous marriage, and they were absent from his life for long periods. They only swung into town when they were on the run from their mom. They would stay for a while, until arguments with the dad and his wife turned into free-for-alls. There were arrests and juvenile detentions, and one time a knife fight. The narrator had me holding my breath by the end. He grew up in a big, luxurious house, always waiting for these brothers who didn't seem to remember him until they needed a place to stay.

I made some notes on the pages to remind myself of what to put in my written critique, especially that the story was honest. Then Pan came in.

"How's business tonight?"

"Dry as a desert." Then I whispered, "Tammie scared off our only potential buyer."

"She's got a shrewd head for business. She ought to invest in DVDs."

"She makes me crazy sometimes."

"Let's pretend she's already gone home," he said. "What have you been up to, beautiful?"

"Reading Caspar Phillips's story. It was excellent."

"Hmm."

"I'm not kidding."

"Doesn't he play football?"

"You bigot. Although I thought the same thing."

"And?"

"You've heard him in class. He's smart. A little slow on the draw, but smart."

"What was so great about it?"

I explained it to him.

"We'll see. I'll read it before I go to bed."

"James, hi." It was Tammie.

"Hey," Pan said. "How are things? Great hair, by the way. Wow."

Tammie smiled like she had been elected May Queen.

"Thank you. Nia, don't get so dreamy-eyed looking at James that you miss customers coming into the store."

"It's hard for me to concentrate," Pan said, "with all these pretty women around." Tammie's flirtatious giggle made me turn and grab the bottle of cleaner to wipe down my counter.

"'All these pretty women,'" I mocked when we got outside. "Are you queer or not?"

"I like to make people happy. Look how she lights up. Besides, she's less likely to kick me out of the store when I need to hang with my real best girl."

He was right.

"I think you're going to be surprised by Caspar's story," I said.

"Maybe."

"It's the best one I've read so far."

"What?"

"Besides yours."

"Quick yet clumsy recovery. Are you sure it was his you

read? He talks like his vocal cords are in reverse."

"I know, but if you listen to what he says, he's got a brain."

"But listening takes patience. I don't have much of that."

I felt defensive and wasn't sure why. "It's a good story, Pan."

"I said I'm going to read it later," he said. "But I don't want to give him the benefit of the doubt. And I don't want you to, either. He's probably like the rest of his buddies. And we know what they think of me."

~

That next Monday in class I made a positive remark about Caspar's piece, even though I hated talking in big groups. I had reread it and still liked it, seen things I hadn't the first time. Pan looked at me once with a wry smile, but he didn't comment at all. Meanwhile, Samsonite, in retaliation for Caspar's betrayal, said, "Dude, there's a lot of run-on sentences."

I looked at Pan, waiting for a smirk, but he didn't seem to be paying attention.

"Where?" Mrs. Burrell jerked her head like she had picked up a scent. "I didn't notice."

Samonsite read a sentence from the piece aloud.

"That's not a run-on, Boz," Mrs. Burrell said. "That's a long sentence. There's a difference."

Then she wrote the whole thing on the board and showed us the grammar.

Trying to save face two classes in a row, Samsonite said, "It's too long. It's hard to pay attention."

"That may be, for you," she said. "But it's not a run-on."

That worked. He sat back in his seat.

After class Pan said he was going to the bathroom and would meet me at the front entrance. I must have packed up too slowly because I was one of the last people in the room. The other person was Caspar.

"I loved your story," I said. "It was really emotional." I wished I hadn't opened my mouth. That had not sounded intelligent.

"Thanks," he said, and looked down at his pack.

Maybe I'd insulted him. I started to leave, embarrassed to have been so gushy and gotten such a laconic response.

"It took me a long time."

I looked back at him, no idea what to say.

"I felt like it was agonizing work," he said. "I must have rewritten it ten times, and then I still wasn't sure. Maybe that's it. You're never sure."

He was looking at me now, pulling at his pack. He had very nice eyes. A light shade of brown. I hadn't noticed them before, probably because his hair tended to hang in front of them.

"Yeah, uh, I know what you mean," I said. "I thought it would be simple at first. But when I got started, I didn't want to do it at all."

Again he didn't respond. Again I turned to go. Then when too many silent seconds had passed, he said, "Yes, that's exactly it."

Every word was deliberate, as if he were translating from another language. I began to say something, but he wasn't done.

"But at the same time, I felt like it was a baby. You can't leave a baby alone. You have to take care of it." That was a strange comparison, but I was intrigued. I didn't know if he wanted to talk more or if I should really go this time.

"See ya," I said, which sounded absurdly out of place.

All I heard, or thought I heard, was him saying something like "Huh."

When I met up with Pan for our walk home, he said, "What are you up to?"

"What do you mean?"

"The look on your face."

I shook my head. I was sure there was no look on my face. I don't know why, but a feeling of resignation came over me as we walked.

"Pan, maybe I should try girls," I said.

"Not following your logic, Nia. But don't worry. You'll find someone. Just not a Mungers Millsian. I mean, what kind of pickings are there here?"

"None, I guess."

"Maybe less than that. You must never, ever date anyone from this town. Except me. That's final."

"But even if I couldn't stand him very long, at least I could say I'd had a date."

"I think it's better to be picky. Maybe a guy from out of town would be worth the effort."

"What town? Look at the names of the towns around here."

"That's true," he said. "Netherford. Who came up with Netherford?"

"Or Triangle Center?" I said. "What about Root? Do you think I can find a quality boyfriend in a town called Root?"

"I would guess not."

"So it's hopeless."

"It's not easy for either of us. What do you think it's like for me living in a place like Mungers Mills? What exactly is a munger, anyway?"

"I don't know. Probably we learned about it in fifth grade."

"It doesn't bother me that much, being single," he said. "I've got you, and I've got Mama Fazzino to cook for me.

What else could a boy ask for?"

"But you do find people. You told me about that guy you met online. And that one you met in Cape Cod, the romance of your life with some Portuguese kid."

"He never answered my texts, if that helps any. A Portuguese ghost."

"But you had sex with him for two weeks."

"Not nonstop. A boy needs to sleep."

"When we went on vacation a few summers ago, before Paolo was born, I didn't get any meaningless sex. I got sun poisoning. And sand fleas."

"Well, souvenirs."

"Do you see how unfair life is? You are gorgeous and blond and thin, which makes it easy for you to find someone. And you get to go on vacations."

"Speaking of the Cape, we're making plans to go for Memorial Day."

"I thought you were going to Florida."

"That's spring break. Those tickets are already bought. But we all want you to come with us to Chatham at the end of May. The pharmacy can spare you."

"I'll think about it. But what'll I do while you're playing with another kid in the changing hut?"

"I exaggerated. I only saw that Portuguese guy a few days. But I did see all of him. He was terrified of his parents finding out. Or of any of his friends seeing us together."

We had reached his house by now.

"So think about it, really. You've got two months to get ready. Mother and Kevin have said a hundred times they'd like me to invite a friend. So that I'll be less sullen."

"Maybe," I said, though I had already decided that if there was any way I could afford it, I would go.

Chapter 11

Imagine being on your own little float making your way along the water, and you look up to see that an ocean liner is coming your way. At first you think that it must see you, that it will at any second make a slow and steady turn. But it keeps getting closer. And you keep waiting for it to veer off, at least enough for a near-miss. Seconds before it's about to plow into you, it stops. You wait because you cannot ignore an ocean liner. That's what it was like that next Wednesday, April Fools' Day, during lunch when Caspar Phillips came toward our table with his tray and a look in his eyes like he didn't know who was navigating.

"Do you mind if I sit here?" he asked with that hard-to-believe voice. "Just for today?" From this angle his face was as innocent as a little boy's, despite the boulder of a body beneath.

"Uh, no," I said, "go ahead." He proceeded to situate himself. Pan looked incredulous.

"I really appreciated the comments you made about my story the other day," he said. It wasn't exactly clear who he was talking to since he was looking between me and Pan, but

I was the only one who had spoken in class about it.

"Yeah," I said, "it was really good." I pretended to keep eating.

Caspar turned his head slightly to Pan. "Some of the comments were okay, but I feel like Nia's really helped."

"Thanks," I said. Pan would mock me later for blushing, but I couldn't help it. "You're a good writer."

"I don't know about that," he said, and kind of smiled. "To tell you the truth, that's the first story I've ever written."

"Same with me."

"The first thing I've ever written that I cared so much about. Most of the time I do the assignment and turn it in and worry about my grade. But this time all I cared about was whether I was going to like it or not. Like I was painting a picture that was going to hang in my house for a long time, so I had to do the best I could."

Then he saw Pan looking at his Apple watch and trying to stifle a yawn. Caspar stiffened, and his face got even more expressionless. "I'm sorry. Were you having a private conversation? You didn't seem to be talking much. My mistake."

"It's okay," I said. "We weren't talking about anything important."

"No," said Pan, "nothing."

"Oh, okay," said Caspar. "So it's nice to find out how other people approached the assignment."

"I approached it from behind," Pan said.

"What?"

"Nothing."

"James," he said, "I think you are an excellent writer. Way beyond the rest of the class."

I think Pan actually blushed this time, then bit on his straw.

"I'm not as good as you," Caspar said, "but I wonder if I have an aptitude for English that I didn't know about."

"You've definitely got talent," I said.

"I've always been good at science."

"And football," Pan added.

"Yeah," Caspar said, possibly missing his tone. "I would like to say football is my favorite subject of all, if only it were a subject. But then too many people would get credit who didn't deserve it."

I couldn't help giving Pan a sardonic smile. Caspar continued as if there weren't something else going on.

"Math comes to me with little effort. But I might go into political science. I guess my politics have always tended to lean toward the liberal side."

I'd never thought about which way my politics leaned.

"I really like science, too," he continued, "but I've never felt excited like I did in English these last few weeks. Well, not excited exactly, because like I told you before, I was in the middle of my story and I just wanted to get out. I didn't enjoy it. It was like being haunted. Possessed, maybe. I've never felt that kind of emotion about a math problem."

"I've been haunted by plenty of math problems," I said.

"There's some kind of trap to making up a world you've based on real life," he said. "It makes you feel like you're inside of it."

I didn't know what that meant, but I thought I could listen to him all day. He didn't say things for filler.

Pan got up. "I'll see you tonight," he said to me. "I've got my physical, like I told you, so I'm getting out early."

"Bye," I said. He left me and Caspar sitting looking at each other. Rather, I looked at him and he looked somewhat to the left of me. The noise from the cafeteria was conspicuously loud compared to our table.

Finally, finally, Caspar formulated a new sentence. "Your friend doesn't like me, I guess."

This was probably true, but Caspar sounded so vulnerable that I had to make up an excuse.

"He's very shy," I said.

"But he talks in class."

"Yeah, but you know, the guys give him a hard time. Really just a few of them. Most people leave him alone." He sat with that. I was learning that when Caspar went silent, he was thinking, not bored.

"I suppose if I were in his position, I would feel the same way. Anyway, I hope I didn't spoil your lunch."

"No, not at all," I said, though it was plain I'd not eaten anything since he'd dropped anchor.

"Okay, then, would you like to go out with me sometime?"

I might have been less startled if he'd asked for my bra.

"What?"

"I'm sorry."

"No, it's okay ...."

"Have I offended you? That's not what I had in mind at all."

"No, no, it's that ... nothing. You took me by surprise is all."

He grinned. He was very handsome when he smiled. "Will that help my cause? The element of surprise?"

"I guess."

"I don't mean to put you on the spot. Do you work on the weekends?"

"At Polaski's. Downtown. Weeknights, too."

"I can give you my number if you want, and you can take some time to think about it."

My impulse was to say yes. Saying no was like turning down a lottery win. I was about to respond when a tiny mosquito of paranoia bit me. There was no evidence for it, but since he did sit with that table of jerks, possibly he had been put up to this: I hung around with Pan. I wasn't one of the babes. No one had ever asked me out before. And it was April Fools' Day. I thought of my thick hair pulled back in an unimaginative braid. Then I could almost see the reflection of my dad staring back at me from the tabletop.

"So," he continued, "put it in your phone?" His insistence made me want to squash the mosquito.

"That's okay," I said, surprised that my voice still worked. "I don't have any minutes left. Uh, I have to see my guidance counselor." That was two lies in as many seconds. I got up and grabbed my lunch bag.

Caspar leaned back a little, looking straight ahead, a snowman's face melting into confusion.

"Uh, bye," I said.

"Yes." His voice rumbled in his chest. "Good-bye."

I took a quick look at the jock table. Not one of them was paying attention to us.

"Thanks," I said, no idea why.

He turned his head to me and those beautiful eyes were cloudy with hurt, but I couldn't go back now.

"For what?" he asked.

"Nothing. I mean, see ya."

"Sure."

I was in the hall so fast that I had no time to figure out where I was really going.

~

That night I couldn't concentrate on work. A couple of people from the residences came in, and I was patient, if not particularly friendly. Tammie snapped at a woman named Edith, who lingered over the body washes too long.

"She's okay, Tammie," I said. "I'll take care of things." I

didn't know if it was the injustice or my irritability making me say it. Either way, Tammie gave me her frigid smile and disappeared. I felt completely dismal when Pan came loping in.

"Kiss me, Kate," he said, leaning over the counter. For some reason I didn't want this kind of playing tonight. "So, did you have a proper din-din, or do I have to go down to Samantha's Fried Chicken and get you a bucket with the bad LDLs? I just got an all-okay from the doctor, so I can eat whatever I want until next year."

"I had something at home ...."

The front door opened and Caspar Phillips came in. Bewildered, I thought that possibly Caspar was related to Tammie somehow, though she had never mentioned any relatives. Before I could unjumble my thoughts, he came straight to me.

"I'm very sorry for being so abrupt today," he said. "In the cafeteria."

"That's okay."

"You see, I tend to work out a situation in my head for a long time before I say something. So I forget that when I'm ready to say it, the other person isn't necessarily ready to hear it."

Pan coughed. Caspar slowly turned to him. Caspar was an inch taller and I don't know how many inches beefier.

"Was I interrupting another conversation?" he asked. "I didn't mean to."

"No," I said. "You don't have to apologize."

"As a matter of fact, I do. That was really inappropriate. I asked my dad about it, and he said that my intention was good but the execution was off."

"What are you talking about?" Pan asked.

"You don't ask a girl out in the middle of talking about

something else," Caspar said. "You've got to lead up to it."

Pan drew back.

"It's okay," I whispered. It wasn't—nothing was. I had to get them out of here. I could pull the fire alarm or hit the panic button under the counter. Tammie's impeccable timing made things even worse.

"Isn't this nice, Nia. You're surrounded by admirers tonight." She followed with an exaggerated sigh. "A girl should be so lucky. But boys—and I hate to sound like the pushy grown-up—if you're not here to purchase a product, you'll have to be going. No loitering. You can read the sign." She looked around for a sign to that effect, and not finding one, turned back. "Those are the rules."

Pan didn't even try to flatter her, just left. Caspar stared at nothing for a few seconds, and then looked back at me. "I've made a big mess. Now I've gotten you in trouble at work, too." Big as he was, he left without a sound.

Tammie raised her eyebrows at me almost imperceptibly, then turned and went back to the office.

Chapter 12

When I got home, it was nine thirty. Pan usually called me late, but that night, nothing. And I didn't have the nerve to call him. I don't know why I hadn't told him about Caspar asking me out—I just hadn't wanted to. And I had said no to Caspar, sort of, by running away like a hen zapped by an electric fence. But the agitation was driving me nuts, and at ten, a much less acceptable hour, I called Pan's cell.

He answered with, "You have exactly thirty seconds to explain."

"People with manners say hello," I said.

"Not in the age of caller ID. No more stalling. I'm plugging in the cattle prod I'm going to use on you. Or him."

"That's what Father Francis always said at Holy Redeemer."

"You actually had a priest in Catholic school? I thought they were extinct."

"He almost was. He was about ninety. And he was always threatening us with a cattle prod."

"Speaking of cattle, explain Caspar asking you out."

"Which one is the cow in this scenario?" I asked, annoyed.

"Me?"

"I would smite anyone who compared you thus."

"Speak English. You're in Munger's Mills now."

"You speak English, Nia. No more stalling."

"He asked me out. Is it so unbelievable that someone might do that?"

"No, not a bit. Any one of those trogs would be lucky to have you for a girlfriend."

"So what are you so mad about?"

He laughed. "Mad? Is someone feeling just a wee bit paranoid? Do you need some of my mother's medications?"

"You said he was a cow."

"Boys can't be cows."

"Come on."

"Okay, I apologize. I don't have anything bad to say about Caspar. Nothing good, either. Now wait—don't get dizzy again. I just mean I don't know him. That's all. But let's examine the real issues. There are two. One is that he had the audacity to move in on you without my permission."

"So you are angry."

"Two is that you hid it from me for hours and hours."

"I was going to tell you, I swear."

"So out with it. What did he say? Word for word. I want exact syllables."

"It's not that dramatic."

"The prod, Missy Parochial School."

"He's kind of blundering, Caspar is," I said.

"Kind of. He never gets a joke, either. You could tell him your brother was a marmoset and he'd consider it."

"We talked a little about homophobia—that is, after you disappeared."

"Homo—What do they even think that means in this town? Fear of houses?

"Honest. He was talking about how hard it must be in our school for you."

Pan was quiet for a moment. "That works in his favor. But he may just have been trying to get into your pantaloons."

"In the cafeteria?"

"Boys will be boys."

"Can I finish?"

"Go."

"So we're talking about that, and then, like he pulled it out of the sky, he asks me if I want to go on a date."

"With him?"

"No, Pan, with a marmoset. Of course with him."

"And you said no?"

"I said I had to go see my guidance counselor."

"Hmm ... innovative."

"For a second, a billionth of a second, I thought that he was doing this for the sake of his friends. The guys he sits with. You know, like on TV when the ugly girl gets asked out by the football captain, and she falls for it, and everyone laughs?"

"That's as much as I needed to hear, Nia. My grandmother must have a grenade in her jewelry case."

"No. That wasn't it at all. I was completely wrong. Maybe because I've watched too much bad TV. Or because no one's ever asked me out before. He's too nice ... honest, or something."

"Or maybe subconsciously you knew he wasn't your type."

"I don't know what my type is, so neither does my subconscious. No, I was wrong. He was asking me for real. I looked over at that table of clowns and they didn't even realize he was gone. Don't you think they'd be sneaking looks and doing all that obnoxious stuff guys do when they're watching a good show?"

"So?"

"So, I'm an idiot. I shouldn't have been so abrupt with him. And then tonight when he came in, I didn't make things any better standing there like a coat rack."

"What were you supposed to do? Tammie Eye Shadow was throwing us all out."

"I could have spoken up. That's two times in one day he's been snubbed. He doesn't deserve that. I think he's an okay guy."

"Wait. Let me rewind one itsy-bitsy second. Am I hearing that you don't care that I got thrown out, only that Caspar did?"

"I didn't say that."

"Yes you did, and I intend to let my feelings be hurt, but not until after we discuss issue number three."

"You said there were only two issues."

"I'm in advanced math. Number three is you really want to go out with him. Now that you know he wasn't fooling, you are actually considering it."

"Oh, all right. So what if I do want to go out with him? He's got beautiful eyes."

"So does a gray wolf."

"There are other things. He's kind of sweet, and a girl needs a little romance once in a while."

"I love you for your spirit. I appreciate you the way no straight guy can."

"Come on, what's the big deal? So he asked me out, and if I weren't such a mushroom, I might have been okay about it. You meet guys and have your little fun."

"Sometimes lots of fun."

"See?"

"But that's different. That's just boys in a hostile land

desperate for affection."

"That could be the title of your next story."

"You wouldn't like it as much as you did Caspar's story, now would you? That's issue number four, the way you raved about it in class."

"Oh, my God, you really are jealous. And if you're going to be this crazy over my one venture into dating—and a date that never happened—then you need to fake being straight."

"Maybe I will. And what's this crap about comparing yourself to ugly girls on TV who get set up by the popular guys? Haven't I taught you anything? You're beautiful."

"Inside."

"No, outside. That's why he asked you out. Not because he's capable of seeing some inner beauty. Boys his age aren't."

"You're a boy his age."

"Quiet. And I'm not saying you aren't innerly beautiful, too. I can see it."

"So, if that's true and he's only after my body, shouldn't I decide if he's worth it?"

I waited. I could hear him breathing, fiddling with something on the other end.

Finally, he laughed, like he had been kidding the whole time.

"If you want to go out with him, then why shouldn't you? He's not a total idiot like his friends. Not even close."

"Really?"

"Don't press me, Nia."

"Okay."

"You have my blessing."

"You sound like somebody's dad."

"I feel like somebody's ex-husband."

"It's too late, anyway. I blew it."

"He'll be back. He's as slow as a caterpillar, but just as persistent. Just remember you are my prom date. I've already bought the trick boutonnière."

"I can't believe you're insecure about that, too."

"So, are you going to call him? Or text your way into his good graces?"

"I don't have his number. I ran away before he could give it to me. I'm going to try to sleep."

"Loves ya."

"Loves ya."

I hung up.

Lying there, I plotted how to tell Caspar that I would like to go out with him after all. But when I had the script worked through, I wondered, What if he's lost interest? What could be more humiliating? Then I had to rewrite the whole thing and focus on apologizing. For myself, then for Tammie. Then if he wanted to repeat his request, I would seize it like a life preserver.

Once I got settled on that course, I remembered how slow Caspar was. What if I apologized, but he didn't understand that he was supposed to repeat the request? An apology wouldn't be enough. I would have to word things so that he grasped my intentions toward his original intentions. But what if my hints were too subtle and I ran out of material before he got it? That required a whole new script, more rehearsal.

I was putting myself out on a frayed tightrope. In the past, I had hinted to other boys that I was available for dating. I might as well have been trying to sell them a *Good Housekeeping* subscription. The last time had been at the beginning of ninth grade, when my imagination had led me to believe Ted Karsinski wanted me for his fall dance date. Only in retrospect could I see what a fool I must have sounded like: asking him if he liked to dance, what his schedule was, what price the tickets were, making a big deal about how the tickets should be free since it was a school activity and we were paying for it with our tax dollars. Really cringe material. Ted avoided me after that. This was one of several small incidents that made me believe I was not date-worthy, at least not at this school. So, though I was anxious to get the invitation from Caspar again, I was just as concerned about avoiding another rejection.

That one potential date had turned into this tightrope act was ridiculous, but I couldn't get myself off it. When I was so tired I couldn't go at it anymore, I fell asleep for what was left of the night.

By morning I was in such a daze I had to keep reminding myself that it was in fact a school day, and I had in fact done my homework. Nerves and fatigue were making me dizzy. I couldn't have been shakier if I'd been about to give a speech. I'm sure I looked like a wreck. I might not survive this almost-dating thing.

Pan was no help. He pestered me in every class we had together, and even threatened to ask Caspar himself.

"Although there's the possibility he'll want to go out with me," he said. "I've never been with a certifiable jock."

"You wouldn't dare," I said. I was overcome by a deep yawn.

At lunch Caspar did not come over to our table, and I tried hard not to look in his direction. In English his face hung like he had been drugged. When Mrs. Burrell called on him, he said, like a proper old man, "I apologize. I seem to be lost in thought today." Something about the way he said it made the class laugh.

Pan waited for me to pack up after, but I sent him off. Since Caspar was lagging behind as usual, this was my chance. If another day went by, I would lose my nerve, and I might worry myself into never sleeping again.

"Caspar," I said, thankful that Mrs. Burrell had left the room. At first he didn't move at all. This worst scenario—that he wouldn't even speak to me—seized my throat. I had no plan for his indifference, but I forced myself on.

"Caspar?"

He turned his head toward me. "Oh, hello, Nia. I hope I didn't get you into too much trouble last night. I wasn't aware I was loitering."

"Loitering? No," I said. "That's my manager. Assistant. She likes the sound of her own voice. You—you two—didn't do anything wrong. You can come." The weight of my ineptitude made my knees buckle. "To the store."

"Thanks." It sounded final.

I could barely remember my lines, but I had to get through this. "So I'm the one who needs to apologize."

"Apologize? For what?" He looked at the floor as if the patterns puzzled him.

"For yesterday. In the cafeteria?"

His expression didn't change.

"When you, you know, sat with us? Me and Pan. James? We were talking about the stories we wrote?"

He looked up at me, his face relaxed back to the drugged look, and he stared just long enough for me to fear he might drool.

"I know. I was very crass."

"No, not at all. I was the crass one. I shouldn't have been so rude like that. It's just that I was surprised, is all."

"Oh, I see."

Then the words sneaked out: "I would love to go out with you."

A mistake, I was sure. I should have stuck with the script,

feeble as it was.

But his brown eyes recharged. A slight smile lifted his big face.

"You would?"

"Yes, sure. Anytime. I mean, not right this minute since we're in school and all."

"My schedule only includes spring track these days. When would be a good time for you?"

I couldn't think of anything, not one single thing, never mind when I was free. Then my identity came back to me. "Saturday nights are good for me. I don't work," I said. Usually I spent them with Pan, but he would be okay for one night.

"Why don't we exchange numbers. Can I walk you to your locker?"

"Yeah, sure."

He stood up. He was easily a foot taller than me. Wider by a person. He had on a light cologne. As we walked through the hall I thought how it would be nice to put my arm around him. It remained a thought. From a distance behind I heard Pan sneeze an amplified sneeze, but I couldn't turn around. When we got to my locker, I looked up at Caspar.

"Thanks," I said.

"May I call you tonight?"

"That would be great."

Before I could see that ocean liner coming at me again, he leaned down and kissed me, lightly, on the cheek. Then he smiled like he had no confidence at all, turned, and walked off.

My body was vibrating.

I tried three times to get my locker combination right. Then Pan was there, pushing me out of the way.

"Here, I'll do it." He opened it, and I grabbed for things

without any purpose. I shut the door, tried to be casual.

"You look like you just saw a fairly large ghost," he said. I mustered a laugh. Pan put his hands on my shoulders. "Welcome," he said, "to the world."

Chapter 13

I had to work that night, and of course I would leave my phone at home in my rush to get out of the house. I called from the store phone and instructed my mom not to let Dad answer it.

"Who are you expecting?" she asked. "Another boy, besides James?"

"Just give him my number here, please. His name is Caspar. It will show up in the ID."

"Interesting name. I might need to talk to him a little," Mom said. "See if I approve. Show him we're friendly."

"No," I said, almost in a shout. Then, more calmly, added, "Please."

"Your dad might want to have a talk with a boy who wants to date his little girl."

"His little girl will not appreciate that."

"What's he like?" Mom asked.

"Questions later. Do you understand what to do?"

"I guess so," she said.

"Do not engage with him. Just give him the number."

"Nia, why are you so nervous?" Mom asked.

"This may be my only call from an interested guy, ever," I said.

"Nonsense," she said. "You've got rich lady's skin."

I felt my eyes tear up. My wonderful, dopey parents loved me like I was something special. I cleared my throat so she wouldn't be able to hear what I was choking back. "I've got to get back to work."

Mom didn't disappoint me, because Caspar never called. Every time the phone rang at work, I jumped for it. Once it rang when I was checking out some customers and I almost turned away from them to grab it. But it was not Mom and it was not Caspar. Pan called twice. Usually I loved to hear from him, but tonight I had trouble paying attention.

"Are you trying to get rid of me, young lady?" he asked during the first call.

"No."

"I know when I'm being tolerated."

"Okay, yes. I can't help it. I'll call you just as soon as I hear from him."

"You'd better."

"I will."

"We'll squeal like little imps."

"Good-bye."

"And Nia Maria?"

"What?"

"When you two get married, I will not call him my brother. Or Dad."

I hung up.

He called back again an hour later, but when there was no news, he didn't try to keep me. He sounded worried himself.

The whole shift went by, and the call never came. There must have been some screwup at my house. When I got home at nine thirty, everyone was in bed. My phone showed no calls from Caspar. Mom looked into my room when I had just turned off the light.

"How was work?" she whispered. We always whispered when Paolo was asleep, the silence so fragile.

"Not bad. We had a little business tonight."

"Your phone didn't ring. Your dad and I kept an eye on it all evening."

"Thanks, Mom. It's okay. He's kind of an airhead. He probably forgot. I'll talk to him in school tomorrow." I attempted to yawn indifference, but I could feel that tears would sneak out if I did.

"That's it, I'm sure. Boys your age are scatterbrained. Except James. Good night."

"Night."

Nothing could comfort me in that dark hour, though I tried to reason away the dread of school the next day. I was pretty sure that on Fridays Caspar was only in one class with me—English—and I could avoid him for forty-five minutes. Then the weekend would come and go, giving me time to build up resistance.

What a relief Friday morning not to see Caspar anywhere in passing, and then in English to find he was absent. By Monday I would be strong again, and I could even smile and say hello to him as if there were no backstory.

Pan was a different story. I wouldn't be able to fake anything with him. During my restless night I hadn't had the energy to think about how he was going to take it. All the way to school he chided me for not calling him before I went to bed. Then he said, "I believe Mister Caspar needs to be punished. How does a bullring sound? We get him drunk, pierce his nose, and he goes through life getting harassed at airport security."

"Between best friends," I said, "I have a request. This

situation goes no further than you and me."

"Of course. Who am I going to tell?"

"I'm just saying, if you start something with him, he's going to know it got to me. It's going to look like I put you up to it."

"Up to what?"

"To whatever. I like my humiliations private. Please don't say anything to him or anyone."

"Tell me this: How will he learn if we don't spank him?"

"He probably forgot. You know how he is."

"He stood up my best girl, that's what I know."

"Making it worse."

"I'm not making it worse. I'm making it right."

"Please."

"All right, then, silence to Caspar. But I'm not sure he'll know the difference. He could be a sheepdog with that hair in his eyes. He doesn't seem to know where he is most of the time."

"Enough about him."

I wanted to call in sick to work that night. I never took time off, because it was hard for Tammie or the owner to get someone else on short notice. But I didn't want to be there. I wanted to stay home, sulk, get back my strength. What a waste to have worried myself into convulsions, making sure I phrased my apology just right so Caspar would ask me out again. And I was annoyed with him in advance for any excuse he might make.

Still, a persistent blip of hope kept squiggling through my mind. Why had he made the special effort to come to where I worked? Then the hope would be stomped by confusion: Why, so quickly, had he forgotten about me? I knew guys could lose interest in girls as soon as they'd gotten what they wanted. Had Caspar skipped that step and gone straight to the dumping?

I went to work anyway. Tammie was sure to explain in detail her boyfriend plans for the weekend. When I got there, though, there was something comforting about being back to normal after the emotional squalls of the past two days. Maybe this was my future: working on a Friday night, looking forward to seeing Pan, hearing about his adventures when he had them.

Just when sorting greeting cards made me stop thinking for a few minutes, Caspar walked in. Actually, I didn't know how long he was behind me before he said something.

"Nia, I've had a rough time."

I spun around. "Hi," I yelped. I was not ready for this. I hadn't planned to be strong until Monday.

Caspar kept his voice low. He remembered that much at least. "My dad had a heart attack Thursday," he said. "I found out when I got home from school. A myocardial infarction."

"Sounds bad," I said, though it really sounded kind of dirty.

"Yes, it was. He had to go in for emergency angioplasty."

"Oh, okay. What's that?"

"It's really an interesting procedure."

"It is?"

"They use an instrument that's kind of like a balloon to unclog the artery. Then the blood can pump like it's supposed to."

"Oh, that. Yeah."

"It's actually fascinating," he said, as if it were not his own dad getting the balloon.

"Is he all right?"

"Things look okay right now. He's in Holland Park at the medical center. It was pretty successful, the procedure, and the cardiologist believes there wasn't a lot of damage."

I didn't want his dad to be sick, but this was an incredibly good excuse.

"I don't know if you remember," he said, "but I told you I was going to call Thursday night."

"Um, yeah, I think you did."

"Oh. Maybe I hadn't said Thursday night. It's quite a blur to me now after all that's happened."

"I can imagine."

"I was worried you would think I was rude or unreliable or something like that."

"No, no," I said. "Of course not."

"It was hard for me to leave my mom through all of this."

"That's where you needed to be. Don't worry about me," I said, then added stupidly, "I got over it."

"I was very worried. Even with my dad sick, I kept thinking how I didn't want to ruin my chance to go out with you."

I could forgive him anything.

"Are you still interested?" he asked.

"Yes," I said too vigorously. "I mean, sure. When your dad gets better, and all."

"I was thinking about tomorrow night, like we talked about in school. Or at least I think we talked about Saturday night. I sound disoriented." He sighed. "Because I am."

"You've got good reason to be," I said, wanting to put both my arms around him.

"Would you like to see a movie? I know the theater here is not great. I have better movies at home. But it's something to do."

"Are you sure? With your dad in the hospital so far away?"

"My mom thinks I should go out and have some fun after

all this. Try, anyway. I really would like to see you."

"Then let's do it."

We stood and looked at each other, then away. We looked at the ceiling, the aisles of products, the floor. One of us was going to have to make a suggestion.

"Let's check the listings and see what's playing," I said, walking to the register and grabbing my phone. I tried to be cool, touching the screen deliberately. I wasn't concentrating on the task, but on Caspar being inches from me.

"Look for the Now Playing button," he said, no impatience or sarcasm in his tone.

"That's right," I said as if I'd just remembered. I found the movie schedule. A rom-com started at 6:40 Saturday at The Moving Picture. We agreed to meet at 6:15 to be sure to get seats. That would give me exactly one and a quarter hours to get home, clean up and change, and get back. I would have to get a ride. Pan might drive me, but that could be awkward. Dad or Mom could give me a ride, but they would ask questions. I could walk, if I ran. I'd figure something out.

"You'd better show up," I said, and smiled.

"You bet I will," he said, and bent and kissed my cheek again. It was just a peck, but I hoped Tammie saw it.

Chapter 14

Having had it withheld from me for so long, I expected dating to be magical, mysterious, different from going out with a friend. But expectation and reality were not twins, in this case.

To start, Mom gave me a warning: "Don't make a big deal if it's not the best night of your life. Just enjoy yourself. You're young. You've got many, many years of dating ahead of you." As if that wasn't curse enough, she added, "Most first dates don't result in any long-term relationship."

Dad had been her first date, but I didn't remind her.

She dropped me off, but I didn't let her stay to meet Caspar, because she was wearing her head gear. Caspar came out of the theater, having bought our tickets. We didn't have much to say, so we went in. I hadn't been to The Moving Picture in such a long time that I'd forgotten how old and run-down it was. Nobody escaped from Mungers Mills alive without knowing it was an old vaudeville theater, whatever that meant, but it had something to do with live shows. Mom had told me that when she was young, a man playing an organ would rise out of the floor in front of the screen. It was terrifying when she was a little girl, but as teenagers, she and her friends thought it was corny.

Caspar and I watched the trailers without a word between us. Then the movie began. Throughout the show I was expecting something to be happening in the audience as well as on the screen, something between us. I would have settled for some conversation. I would lean over to remark about this or that happening on-screen, and he would nod, very minutely. That's all. After three tries I quit, but I looked at him a few times to see that his lips were parted as he watched the screen with strict concentration. He might have forgotten me. I felt homesick for Pan, who was on a date of his own. He and I whispered our own narrations during bad movies—much like we did when we watched TV in his room—until we provoked people around us and stopped. We mixed candy and popcorn for the effect of salty and sweet. He would put his lean arm around me, and I'd snuggle against him.

Caspar, by comparison, was like one of those Easter Island monuments. His mammoth shoulders and torso, which I had found quite attractive earlier in the evening, spilled over into my space. If he was going to touch me, it should at least be inappropriate. But he was so still that at one point I was sure he had stopped breathing. That would be a story—finding my first date dead when the lights came up.

The movie was all right, when I paid attention, but mostly I sat and analyzed what was not happening, how our evening wasn't even approaching magical. I was supposed to be sexually charged, and instead I was fantasizing about organic mac and cheese with naturally cured ham chunks at Pan's house. When the credits started, I jumped up, conceding failure. My life wasn't bad the way it was: I had an okay job and a roof over my head, and a handsome best friend with lots of money who adored me. Who needed this?

Caspar sat and watched every name roll up, to the last gaffer and best boy. I had to sit back down. Finally, the lights went up.

"I didn't think that plot was very credible," he said, turning as much as he could.

He was alive, and he did remember me after all.

"I don't know," I said, trying to recall.

"Remember what Mrs. Burrell said in class? If you set up a certain logic, you have to stick with the logic throughout your story."

"Yeah."

"Yes, they have broken a cardinal rule here. They wanted something to happen, so they forced it to happen, even if it didn't make sense."

He was starting to interest me, like he did in class. It could be that Caspar operated in gears. When he was in, say, first gear, he was nearly catatonic. Then he upshifted, and slowly you realized he was not only animate but intelligent. He never got into overdrive though. Maybe on the football field. But I had not yet seen him excited or agitated or quick.

"What did you think of it?" he asked.

"I agree," I said.

"You don't have to. People have many different interpretations. That's just how I see it."

"I wasn't paying as much attention. To the logic, that is. It was a typical rom-com."

"Yes, that's it. The usual Hollywood stuff. Big romantic reconciliation at the end. You can let something slide if the story is entertaining."

"I might not be smart enough to know better," I said.

He put his nearest hand on mine, and held it there.

It wasn't like when Pan held my hand. Well, the first few

times I'd nearly passed out, but the electricity had shut off when I knew it was only brotherly love. This was real, and it had been worth waiting for in silence. Caspar managed to maneuver himself so that he could kiss me, a gentle kiss on the lips.

I didn't know what to do next, so I sat there like a display. When he didn't try to kiss me more, I stood up again. Caspar remained seated. I was conscious about lagging behind in an empty theater with the lights on. People would be coming in for the next show soon. Caspar looked up at me—there was not much difference in our heights with him sitting down— and he had such pretty eyes to peer into. He also looked so innocent. He put his hands on my hips and sat me on his knee, and kissed my lips again. It wasn't a comfortable position by any means, an armrest pushing deep into my butt and me twisting to match my lips to his, but I was feeling delirious anyway.

"Time to go, lovebirds," someone called, someone who sounded a lot like Pan, who was supposed to be in Holland Park with an online date. This pulled me back through the levels of delirium. I looked behind us, but no one was there. It had to have been Pan, his voice deep and almost musical, and mildly amused.

"I guess we should go," Caspar said. We made our way out of the theater, his hand in mine. When we got outside, he put his arm around me. I enjoyed this, though I was also afraid the phantom Pan might comment more from the shadows. We walked, neither of us saying anything about which direction we ought to be going.

"I had a great time tonight," Caspar said.

"So did I."

He stopped and went in for another kiss. This time he moved his tongue in, and his mouth was minty. I tried to go with it, but I felt rigid. I wasn't sure how this was done, so I opened my mouth a little. Caspar knew what he was doing, or was good at pretending. It was the strangest sensation, but one that made me curious for more. Years of deprivation made me want to make up for lost time, get too into it and open my mouth too wide, but I let him lead. Caspar was patient, gentle, and constant.

"A so-so movie. But a wonderful girl," he said when we finally broke.

I didn't care that the movie had left me completely now, although he would doubtless bring it up again for discussion. I might have to sneak back and see it on my own to be prepared.

"I should walk you home, Nia."

"Sure. It's pretty far. About a mile or so."

"That's fine with me."

"And we're heading the wrong way."

I turned us around.

When Caspar and I got to my house, my parents were waiting.

Mom bubbled down the porch steps. Her appearance hadn't changed since she'd dropped me off. "You must be Caspar. I'm Nia's mom. And this is Mr. Fazzino." Dad stood on the porch like a column.

"Very pleased to meet you," Caspar said, reaching out and shaking her hand. He looked at Dad, whose head might have moved.

"So, did you kids have a good time tonight?" Mom asked.

I gave her a hug. When my mouth was close to her ear, I whispered, "Go inside. Now."

She pulled away from me. "It's been nice to meet you, Caspar. I hope you're taking good care of our girl."

"Mom," I said with a smile she needed to fear.

"Good-night, you two." She turned and went back up the porch steps. Dad nodded faintly, like a mime with arthritis, and went in behind her. The door shut, and the porch light, which had not been on, lit up.

"Mom," I called, loud enough to be heard through the door she was spying behind. The light went off. I was unsettled now. Our front porch looked like a poverty cliché, especially with that socket and bulb hanging from wires. And my parents were playing with the light switch.

"Sorry about them," I said.

"What was your mother wearing on her head?"

"Some kind of hair thing," I said, trying for nonchalance.

"It looked like a do-rag," he said.

I couldn't explain her. "She wears that under her wig."

He looked confused.

"Not really."

"They seem nice, at least your mom. Your dad looked like he was suspicious."

"He doesn't much like boys my age. He's always been really cold to Pan—I mean James. I thought it was because he's gay. But maybe he just doesn't approve of anyone."

"I would really like to see you again. I can't make firm plans right now, though I don't want you to think I'm being rude. My dad is still in the hospital, and I have to wait and see how we're going to schedule things."

"Sure," I said. "Don't worry about me. I'm pretty much always here." That sounded pathetic. "Or at work." That wasn't much better.

But Caspar kissed me, the serious kind, and I loved wrapping my arms around his wide, taut body.

The porch light went on again. I would be wrapping my hands around someone's neck soon. To spite Mom and Dad, I pulled Caspar out of the range of light and resumed kissing him. The light went off and on again. I couldn't tell whether my heart was racing because of Caspar or because soon I was going to be an orphan. I pulled back. I didn't want to stop, but I had to before my parents got the floodlights out.

"How are you going to get home?" I asked. "You're like miles from here."

He pulled out his cell phone and pressed some numbers. He spoke cryptically—quicker than usual—then folded it and put it back in his pocket.

"Uber," he said to me.

I should have gone in and made Dad offer a ride. That would have served him right. But I didn't trust what he would say on the way. And also I felt weird about Dad and me and Caspar riding together, considering how I was feeling.

A car pulled up.

"Good night, Nia," he said, giving me one last, earnest kiss despite an audience of three now.

"Bye," I said as he got in the car. I went into the house, snapping off the porch light as I closed the door.

Mom wanted details, but she wasn't getting them.

"You could have woken Paolo," I said, "with your trotting in and out of the house. And what's with the lights?"

She drew back. Then I felt bad. Her life was so flat, and all she wanted was some girl talk.

"Mom," I said, "I think he's really nice. He's got the sweetest eyes."

"Why don't you invite him in next time?" she asked.

"Maybe. Good night," I said, and went to my room.

Lying on my bed, I let the irritation pass. There was Caspar to dream about.

Chapter 15

Pan called first thing Sunday morning, so I confronted him first thing. He swore it had not been his voice in the theater. I wasn't convinced, but I let him off. I never had the energy to spar with him for long.

When he demanded information about my date, I felt shy, like there was a confidence between me and Caspar that I shouldn't share. Pan interpreted my condensed version as a lack of interest. That worked, for the time being.

"Sounds like it was boring."

"He's nice. Not exactly traditional. As far as conversation, that is. But really nice in his own way."

"Now you're getting defensive," said Pan. "I didn't say he was boring. I said it was boring."

"I have a few questions for you about your little date," I said.

"Not so fast. Are you going out with him again?"

I didn't answer.

"I repeat: Are you going out with Casparino again?"

"Not sure."

"You don't sound thrilled."

"It's not that. He can't make plans with his dad being in the hospital and all. He said he'll call me when he can."

"That old excuse, my father's heart attack. I've used it."

"Your dad's heart did stop," I said.

"Or froze. So in a way I'm being truthful."

"Are you saying Caspar's trying to ditch me?"

"He better not. Mama Fazzino and I will march right over to his house with that cattle prod."

"That's really sweet. Now, how did your date go? You'll notice I'm not interrogating you about your latest boyfriend."

"He's not going to be my boyfriend," he said. "That much of the future I can predict."

"Why? What happened?"

"Nothing much. Nothing good, anyway."

"Was he cute?"

"Yes. In context."

"What?"

"He was old."

"How?"

"Profile said twenty. In person he wasn't. He said people *tell* him he looks twenty. Even though he's thirty-one."

"Oh my God, that's disgusting."

"He even had a few gray hairs. And some missing."

"He knew you were only seventeen and he still went out with you? Isn't that illegal?"

"I don't know. But I wasn't exactly honest, either."

"How?"

"Twenty-one. He was supposed to think I was older than him."

"You shouldn't have."

"It's different than telling people you're younger than you are."

"I'm not following your reasoning here, Pan. Why not just be honest?"

"Because saying 'seventeen' is like a death knell in anonymous dating. Why should I be honest when no one else is?"

"You might meet another boy your own age and actually have fun."

"Someone my own age with a mortgage is what I met."

"I'm afraid you're going to get hurt. Some predator is going to lure you."

"I don't meet them just for sex. It's dating, just like you normal kids."

"I know ...."

"And I can't go making a date with someone in the hall at school like the privileged do."

"You're saying I'm privileged? Me?"

"If it weren't for online dating, there would be no dating."

"I know," I said. "But I worry."

"I won't go home with anyone craggy. I swear."

"What did you wind up doing when he turned out to be ancient?"

"Went to the movie anyway. When we sat down, he asked me how old I was. I told him eighteen at first, forgetting what I had told him online. When I saw how uncomfortable it made him—and because he had lied really bad himself—I played bashful and told him I was really only seventeen. The younger I got, the more he squirmed like his hemorrhoid cream was wearing off. So I just couldn't help but say I was really only sixteen. Or about to be."

"You are cruel. And then?"

"Then he got up and left. He didn't give me a chance to get any younger. He sat there frozen for a second, then stood up and said he needed to use the bathroom. As he tried to get by me, I whispered that my dad was a state trooper."

"He must have panicked."

"He didn't even react, just stepped past me, headed for the bathroom, never came back. I ruined his evening. He wasted mine. Although I noticed you two were having a good time. Eventually."

"I knew it. You spied on me, Detective Pansy."

"At your service."

"I can't believe you."

"What else was I supposed to do? My date left me in the middle of the movie. I had to entertain myself. And I wanted to make sure Caspar didn't go too far."

"Pan, if I didn't love your jealousy so much, I'd end the friendship right here and now."

"I just wanted to make sure my best girl was okay. And weren't you two into each other when the lights went up?"

"I continue to hate you."

"Is he a better kisser than me?"

"How would I know?"

"Don't underestimate me, Nia. I'm already plotting to get you away from Caspar Phillips and make you mine, all mine."

"How much did you see?" I asked.

"Why? Did you go all the way? Right there in the theater? I've done it myself, so I'm not judging."

"You're acting an awful lot like my parents. Minus the sex in public. They were waiting for me when I got home. Wouldn't leave us alone. I was ready to kill them, too."

"They are good people. Taking care of their own. Maybe if you tell your father I chaperoned you, he'll like me a little. Or dislike me less."

That made him sound vulnerable. My indignation melted.

"If it helps any, Dad wasn't exactly a great host with

Caspar, either. He didn't say a word. He just stood there."

"Maybe he thinks Caspar's a homo, too."

"It's not because you're a homo. He doesn't warm up to people fast."

"Fast like an ice age."

"I've got to get ready for work."

"I'll be by to torment you and make your day pass faster," he said. "Especially now that I'm in competition for your affections."

"I will never forgive you, Pan, ever."

"What about now?"

"No."

"Now?"

"Maybe."

"Good enough. Loves ya."

"Loves ya, and good-bye."

Chapter 16

Caspar had invited me over for pizza and a movie Saturday, the night before his dad was coming home from the hospital. He didn't know what things would be like at home after that.

When Mom found out about this second date, she casually brought up the safe-sex rules she had taught me many times before. It was about how my body worked and how a boy's worked and what could happen if they worked together too well.

"Mom, come on. It's just pizza," I said, wanting the lesson over.

But she would not be stopped. She went beyond the basics of being responsible, warning me that the first sex probably wouldn't be that great, that we would be awkward with each other. I might not like some things—positions, sensations, odors.

"Balls," she finally said, to make things worse. "Be prepared for the balls. Just the strangest things."

"Ma." But before I could steer her in any other direction, she continued.

"Here, I want you to have these." She handed me a box of

condoms as if passing down her grandmother's wedding ring. "Very important. These will prevent disease and reduce the chance of pregnancy." From his bedroom Paolo let out a squall. She bit her lip. "When used correctly."

I knew she would be destroyed if I got pregnant and had to save up my meager pharmacy earnings for my wedding reception at the Knights of Columbus hall. She did not want me living her life with all its missed possibilities. I wouldn't. But she was going to spoil any potential magic by turning my second date into a cautionary tale.

I didn't tell Pan about this new date, not immediately, and I felt guilty about it. As he and I made our long trek to his house from school midweek, he asked, "So, what do you want to do this weekend? It's supposed to be spring, although it's taking a long time to get here. This town is behind in everything."

I told him I was taking Mom to a movie Saturday night, which was not a well-planned alibi.

"That's great," he said. "I'll tag along."

Mom would have liked that, had she been going. Then I told him it was girls' night only. He still wanted to come.

"On a Saturday night? You must want to find another date to make up for the bad one."

"With who? I'd rather do your mother a favor. It's better than spending my time with some old geezer." He put his arm around my shoulder.

Before we walked another three yards, there was a knot of guilt in my throat.

"The truth is I have another date."

I felt his arm go limp around me.

"Caspar," I said after a long silence.

"You're a terrible liar, Nia. You sounded fake."

"I don't know why I made that up about Mom. I feel like

I'm cheating on you. Dumb, huh?"

"Trying to spare my feelings."

"I'm sorry. It was stupid."

"He'll have to take you somewhere else," he said. "I'm not sure I can handle another two hours in The Moving Picture."

"Am I still under surveillance?"

"Yes, so please consider my convenience when you make plans with him."

"We're going to his house."

"Oh." More silence, then, "That's not convenient at all."

"I'm sorry, Pan. I really am."

"Are you going to make a man out of him?"

"It's only our second date. He's the first boy I ever kissed. I'm not real forward in these matters, as you know."

"Out with it. Are you planning to do push-ups?"

"I don't know."

"You are. You sound fake again."

"I said I don't know. Why rush it? If he's going to dump me after, I might as well hold out for a few more dates."

"No more of that. I won't listen to you trash the girl I love."

"But—"

"No, enough. If he dumps you, he's the asshole. End of conversation."

It couldn't be the end of this conversation, because I needed his advice, and bad. Mom had taught me the basics, but she hadn't addressed the paranoia I was starting to feel about my body. When we got to Pan's house, I had a list of questions in my head. His grandmother was sitting in the living room. I waved as we sprinted past.

Ada was not around, but Kevin came in the back door while Pan served me an omelet casserole made with free-range eggs.

"Nia!" he said, like I'd been gone for a year. I got up, and he hugged me. "What's new in your life, youngster?"

"Nia's got a boyfriend," Pan said, flat and toneless.

"That's great, honey," Kevin said. "Who's the lucky guy?"

"Uh, Caspar. He's in our English class."

"They've taught you about the chirpies in school, right?"

"Kev, please," said Pan. "Can we talk about the weather?"

"Chirpies?" I asked.

"That's what Kevin calls STIs. Syphilis, gonorrhea, HIV. Chirpies."

"It's a clinical term," Kevin said and winked. "We've got condoms, Nia. We keep them in the downstairs hall closet. James will show you where they are, and you take them if you need them."

"Uh, okay," I said.

"No questions asked. James knows."

"Bye, Kev," Pan said, and Kevin moved toward the doorway.

"See you, urchins. Have a nice snack."

I was touched by Kevin's concern, if not by his discretion.

"Is every adult in this town interested in my potential sex life?" I asked.

"For them it's reminiscing."

When we got to his bedroom, I said, "Listen, Pan, I do need some advice. It's true that it could happen any time for Antonia JoAnne Fazzino. I'd been sure until recently that I would be the only virgin in the retirement community. I know the rules and stuff, and I'm going to do close shaves on my arms and legs. But how do I know when ... you know, if he wants to? If we both want to?"

"I wish I could tell you," he said. "Sometimes you'll be making out furiously and you're sure it's going all the way. And it turns out the other person just wants to make out furiously."

"That doesn't help."

"It's a case-by-case thing, Nee. All I can say is do what feels right. And don't be afraid to run if you change your mind."

"Maybe being dateless was easier."

"Easier but not fun. Don't worry. I'll be by your side through the whole ordeal."

"Ew."

"In spirit."

"Still ew. Pan, the thing is—and I know this should not have astounded me—I realized I would have to be naked in front of him. Like, naked."

"That's usually the drill."

"But I've never ... only in front of the girls in gym, and only when they force us to shower, which they usually don't. I'm not used to that kind of exposure."

"Everyone is that way. It's not just you."

"Everyone? You? You have a beautiful body."

"Yes, and?"

"What do you have to be self-conscious about?"

"You never know, Nia, if the other person is going to like what they see. Doesn't matter what the general consensus is. If the guy isn't into you, he's not into you."

"Thanks a lot."

"No, you're getting it wrong. I'm saying everyone has the same fear. Up until the point of no return, there's some mystery about what the other person looks like in the flesh. So I'm a little nervous too that the guy is not going to like how much body hair I have, or ...."

"Stop right there."

"But you shave your legs, right? It's not like he's going to find a Black Lab. Just relax."

"I'm never going to get this right. What if I smell? Mom said the smells might be peculiar, but what about my smells? They're not strange to me, but what if he's been with other girls before and my, you know, fragrance, isn't what he likes?"

"What if he smells? Have you ever heard of the scrotum?"

"Have you and my mom been comparing notes? She warned me about balls, too."

"It's not a ventilated part of the body," he said.

"He always smells good. Cologne."

"Cologne only works in so many places."

"I'm worried about me, not him."

"You'll be fine. Listen, no one knows exactly what they're doing the first time. And the second time wasn't much better for me, as I recall. It takes a while to get used to each other. But worrying about it is going to make you hate it. You don't want to be like the girl in the movies who cries afterward. Look, Nia, if this were anybody else, I could see why you might be torturing yourself. But it's Caspar. He's not a typical, run-of-the-Mungers-Mill jerk. He's not going to talk about you afterward. Just be yourself. And if by chance he doesn't like this or that, he can either get used to it or get lost. Remember, he's worried about the way he looks, too. And smells. I assume."

He took my hand and led me to the downstairs hall closet, dug through a wall of long coats to the back, and pulled out a strip of condoms. "There are enough here for a water-balloon convention."

"Put them back," I said, looking behind me. "Your grandmother will see them."

"She thinks they're coasters. Now listen. Keep his thing covered up no matter what. You heard what Kevin said: No chirpies. And no babies either. I'll babysit for your sonic brother, but that's it."

"Come on, I'm not going to get pregnant. We might not even do it."

"Here," he said, putting them in my hand. "Take a six pack."

I took them. With Mom's included, I was prepared for a lot of luck. "I'll cherish them always," I said.

"Yeah, don't do that."

I put my arm around him. "Loves ya a hundred times," I said.

"Loves you even more than that. Use the love gloves."

Chapter 17

Saturday night Dad gave me a ride to Caspar's in our truck. He was striped with grease.

"Are his parents home?" he asked.

"His mom and his aunt are," I said, though I wasn't sure they were.

"Did you leave us his number?"

"Yes. Don't worry."

"It's one thing to be hanging around with gay boys. It's another to be going to a guy's house on your own."

"So now you trust James? Before you didn't want him alone with Paolo."

"I wasn't worried. Just concerned."

"What's the difference?"

"A dad wants to protect his kids."

"From what, Dad? It would mean a lot to him if you even cracked a smile. He thinks you hate him. He's my best friend."

"I'll try. It just seems like a waste, you know, a nice-looking boy being like that."

"The nicest-looking boys are like that."

"Be careful tonight, honey. I don't want anyone hurting my baby girl."

"Believe me, I'm loving the fact that you're worried about me going out with a boy because I'm really going out with a boy. Worry more often, will you? Maybe it will get me more dates."

"Has your mom had that little discussion with you about things?"

"Sex?"

"Don't even say it until you're married."

"Uh-huh. She told me how well you two did with that."

He may have blushed under his film of grease.

Caspar lived in the newer part of town, where the cursed Green Goose Day School was located. This was money in a different way from Pan's neighborhood, where rich people had built homes a hundred years ago. Here the houses were big and newish, with enormous yards, swimming pools, campers, and swing sets.

"Here. This is it," I said.

Dad stopped the truck, then looked at me. He tried to put a hand on my face, but I drew back.

"Transmission fluid," I said.

He grinned, a little. "You really are beautiful, you know that? I know you don't think you are."

I blew him a kiss and jumped out. I was ashamed of being ashamed that Caspar would see the truck or catch a glimpse of Dad all greasy.

He waited while I stood at Caspar's front door. I gestured for him to move on. When he didn't, I started toward the truck and finally he drove off. Caspar came to the door wearing a lavender sweater and a pair of black jeans. A second of dizziness hit me.

He showed me inside, then down to his basement, which

was more luxurious than any room in my neighborhood.

"This is kind of my home inside my home," he said. I turned to look at him, and he put his arms around me, bent a little, and kissed my lips. He took my hand and led me to a huge leather couch. We sat down and began some more intensive kissing. I managed to pull away for a second to catch my breath, check my pulse.

"If my dad could see us, he'd have a heart attack," I said. Then I remembered his dad's heart attack. What an idiot. "He was worried about chaperones."

"You're safe with me," Caspar said. "I would never do anything to hurt you."

His eyes were an intense brown, and he looked at me like I was a rare, brilliant diamond. "You are so pretty," he said softly. He almost seemed confused, his mouth open and his eyes transfixed.

He didn't suggest anything else, verbally or otherwise, and went up to get the pizza his mom had ordered for us.

"No beer?" I asked, as he came back down.

"Oh. I don't drink beer. I don't like it. My dad and mom let me have wine once in a while. I could find some of that if you wanted."

"No, no, I didn't really mean it. You know, pizza and beer. Just sort of go together."

"Oh."

"But I didn't really want it. Wine either. Pizza is fine." I stammered on: "Not that I'm going to drink the pizza. I'll chew."

I really just needed to shut up.

He opened a mini-refrigerator in the basement's kitchenette. "We have all kinds of soft drinks. Mainly diet soda. My mom."

"That's exactly what I want," I said. "Cola."

There wasn't much to say as we ate, but every movement either of us made was charged.

After we were done, he opened up the louvered doors of the entertainment center under his mammoth, space-age TV and revealed a bunch of other machines and a library of videotapes and DVDs.

"We love movies," he said. "We have everything listed either by the director or by the genre. My dad never throws anything away and never turns down a streaming service."

For a few moments I forgot the charge in the room as my eyes skipped through titles of movies I had never heard of, actors too.

"It's just that at a movie theatre we can't get the kind of stuff my dad and I enjoy. Like the one we saw last week. He wouldn't pay a dime for that."

"We should have come here instead," I said. That sounded suggestive. Was I going to say anything right this evening? I took out random DVDs and read their descriptions. "A lot of these sound really interesting."

"This is great," he said, picking one up. "But it's in Spanish. Can you stand it?"

"Yeah," I said. "Let's see if my high school education has paid off."

"I mean, it has subtitles, but some people don't like to read them."

I looked up at him and felt pleasantly light-headed again. He looked younger from this angle but so fine that I wanted to put my head on his chest and just hold it against him. As usual, I didn't go with the impulse.

The movie was interesting in a way movies seldom were for me. It had no explosions. I forgot within minutes that I was reading subtitles. Caspar sat close and soon had his arm around me. I sat stiff at first, then relaxed and leaned back into him.

During the closing credits he kissed me. At first the panic came back like an annoying cough and I wanted to pull away and just go home. But Caspar was in no rush, and as he persisted, every touch of my hand on any part of his skin, especially his face, was like vibrating fire. Eventually I let go of all the things that were wrong with me, and I could easily have forgotten how to breathe. We didn't go far, didn't even taken off any clothes, though some buttons were undone. But it was further than I'd ever been.

At some point it was like we both wanted to rest and hold each other. I couldn't get enough of the kissing, or that focused, obsessed look on Caspar's face.

He drove me home in an old, red pickup truck that stood out among all the pricey toys in his yard. It was in even worse shape than Dad's, which was something of a consolation even if it was his family's junky set of wheels.

He was silent as he drove. If this was where he told me it was nice knowing me or that he just wanted to be friends, I could deal with it. It had been an incredible evening and I could live on it for a while.

Instead, he said, "When can I see you again? I'd like to. Or are you going to be busy?"

"I'm free whenever," I said. "I do have a job, but I don't work all the time."

"You might want to think about being my girlfriend," he said in his sluggish, old man's voice.

"I will. I like the idea."

"Not as much as I do."

"Next Saturday?"

"I'll see you Saturday. Besides in school, I mean."

He pulled up in front of my house, which belonged to another lifetime. He leaned over for a last kiss. Neither of us said anything. I hopped out. I knew I wouldn't be able to sleep now that my new life had begun, and that was fine.

Just before I made contact with the first step, the porch lights went on. I loved Mom and Dad, no matter how embarrassing they were. I shook my head and went in.

Chapter 18

I didn't understand why I felt so odd the next morning. I looked around and my room was the same place I had grown up in, the walls needing spackle and paint, my posters curling and lopsided. Yet I might as well have woken up in France. And when Pan called me to demand a transcript of my evening, I felt like I had amnesia. His voice was familiar and strange at the same time. As he talked, I started coming back to myself.

"Nia Maria, you cannot put me off. I knows ya and I loves ya too well. Spill it, baby, spill."

It was no use lying to him, so he was the third person to know about my adventures. But I didn't feel excited about revealing the details, no giggling or breathlessness. It came across flat, like I was explaining a homework assignment. I even sensed that I was boring him, so I turned the subject away from me.

"The first kid I had sex with?" he asked. "Full on?"

"Any level," I said. I had always tried not to sound fascinated when Pan told me of his exploits, although my wanting details gave me away.

"The first time?" he repeated. "I don't know if I can remember that far back."

"Try."

"I remember Justin Holub giving me a piggyback ride when I was in first grade. That was my first of many schools. He must have been in sixth grade, and he looked like a giant to me. I liked it more than he knew. Then he put me on his shoulders."

"What was the first sex you had that the other person was aware of?" I asked.

"Let me think," he said. "Sixth grade."

"You waited that long?"

"That was the year we spent in Vermont. My parents wanted to start camping, but Kevin didn't think he could sleep in a tent. They bought a pop-up trailer and set it up in the driveway. I was friends with Karl Kline, who was a year older than me and this brawny, kind of fat kid. We were best friends that year. I always helped him with his spelling homework. Remember those little workbooks?"

"Get on with it."

"I got to invite him for a sleepover. My parents were unintentionally accommodating."

"So what happened with Karl Kline?"

"I don't remember how we got there, but we were wrestling one minute, and then the next minute we were wrestling a little too tenderly. I was the husband and then he was the husband. We rolled around in one of the bunks and kissed each other like it was a game. Wrestling and rolling, and kissing, and me saying things like, 'Where's my supper?' You know, both trying to be the man."

"I am completely grossed out," I said. "Keep going."

"We fell asleep, and the next morning the game was over and we were back to not wrestling."

"Did you ever play house with your husband again?" I asked.

"Stop panting, Nia. Last night is over. No, nothing else happened. I wanted a rematch, of course. But he didn't, and I don't remember any big scene or tears or fights. Just didn't do it. We moved away, as usual. Never saw him again. Why are you so interested in my love life this morning?"

"I was just wondering because, you know, of my inexperience."

"You're not inexperienced anymore."

"Anyway, I have to go. I have to work all day."

"Wait, Nia, what are you doing next Saturday after work? There's a movie I want to see in Holland Park."

I had made that date with Caspar.

"That's such a long drive," I said.

This evasion was met by silence.

"Hello? Pan?"

"I'm here."

"I thought you hung up."

"I should. What do you mean it's such a long drive? When have you ever cared about how long the drive is?"

"It's just ...."

"I'll drive. I'll pay for the gas, the movie tickets, the candy, and some ruby red shoes if you want."

"It's just that one night I'd like to stay home and rest."

"Then come to my house instead. You can relax, without your brother crying for the moon."

"Uh ...."

"Liar. You're meeting Caspar."

"I am."

"Why not just tell me when you're ditching me? Don't you think it makes it worse to invent these stories?"

"I'm not ditching you. Don't be dramatic."

"Do me a favor and don't try to spare my feelings, okay?"

"You're right. I'll stop," I said. "It's like I'm worried you and Caspar will have to share me from now on." There was a pause.

"How am I going to survive in this town without you?" he asked. "Half these people would burn a cross on my lawn if they could figure out which side of the match to light."

"No they wouldn't. And I'm not going anywhere."

"That's the way it works. A girl gets a boyfriend and she drops her best friend."

"I'm not like that," I said, then stopped. I was like that, able to concentrate on one person at a time. I thought of how I'd not really spent much time with Amanda since Pan came around. "Besides, I don't know how serious ...."

"He wants to see you again, and after a night of passion. That's serious. That's practically engaged in Mungers Mills."

"Pan, it's my first wade into this pool. Let me enjoy it. You get lots of attention from boys. Why not let me have some?"

"I don't have boyfriends," he said, "I have dates. Once they find out I live here, they run like there's a gas emergency."

"Untrue. Lots of boys would be very happy to be your special friend. I think you're the picky one. I think you're the one who's not ready to settle for one person."

"We're discussing your character flaws, not mine. And I never let my love life get in the way of our romance."

"But you might. If you started to date one of those guys for real, you might need to juggle your schedule to keep me in it."

"I'd be truthful if I did."

"I get it," I said. "I'm sorry. Again."

"Tell me how much you loves me and hang up."

"One hundred billion."

"That's all?"

"Good-bye."

Chapter 19

Caspar's dad had not come home from the hospital as planned. The balloon procedure had not been a success after all, and he had to have open-heart surgery. So Caspar was mostly alone in his big house for a few weeks, except when I came over. The second time we were together, I had felt more shy than the first, like I'd used up my charms and he was not going to like me anymore. But he did like me still, peering at me all the while as if I were a psychedelic rainbow.

I would eventually have to bring him around to my house again. But how could I let him see what I lived in, and in the daylight? And what would Mom think of him if they talked for more than the few seconds they had the night of our first date? I was sure she and Caspar would not click. Pan was all personality and charm and she perked right up when he visited. She could easily become his new best friend. She had even slapped Dad down a few times over him.

"What's your problem?" she said one day after Dad rolled his eyes when I said I was walking to work with Pan. "Give it a rest, Tony." That sent him out of the room. But it wasn't going to help with Caspar that Mom was so fond of Pan.

Actually, if not for our meetings at his house, I would barely have seen Caspar at all. We might as well have been in different schools for all that we interacted in that building. The only time we talked was a few seconds in classes here and there. It was strange passing in the hallways and smiling at each other as if we were acquaintances. And even stranger that we didn't discuss this weird, naturally occurring arrangement.

The segregated seating at lunchtime also remained the same. Pan and I would eat together, and Caspar was back at his table. I would sneak a look at him when I thought Pan wouldn't catch me, and see Caspar looking so dismal in all that clamor. Once in a while he would see me watching him and a shy expression would pass over his otherwise lonesome face. I was not going over to that table no matter what, and there was probably some kind of shield Pan was giving off that kept Caspar away from us.

School was out for spring break. Pan was in Key West with his parents. I enjoyed my own small vacation in the suburbs with Caspar, looking out the huge picture window in his room at his endless backyard with its variety of outdoor things—plots for gardens, a seat swing, huge weeping willows. A small artificial pond and an inground swimming pool, even in the bareness of early spring, were more attractive than anything in my bleak backyard. None of us had raked this year, and no one had ever landscaped. I was envious that everything looked so manicured even after winter.

He and I lay together on top of his queen-size bed, another luxury I had not known to long for. We were still not completely intimate, so we weren't naked and under the sheets, but we had graduated from the couch. Conversation didn't make me as anxious now that I was more used to his patterns, which included long pauses. I now found his old-mannish style adorable. I might have been in love with him already, although I didn't know how that was supposed to feel exactly.

I asked him how big the yard was. He considered the question as if it was very important.

"Big enough for a long forward pass," he said, and kissed me. I couldn't believe this same guy was one of the stars of the football team, my lovable hulk with his brooding thoughts. I was being foolish to worry so far in advance, but already I dreaded this coming summer and football practice starting. It began the last week in July, he had told me. Though he'd given me no reason to, I worried about him getting caught up with that crowd, leaving me behind. He would be a senior after all, and for some of his teammates, that was as high as the elevator went. And what were they saying to him about dating me? I felt very insubstantial against them. As for me penetrating that world by, for example, making the cheerleading squad, well, that wasn't happening.

"What's so great about football?" I asked, implying criticism without intending to. "I mean, what do you like so much about it?" That wasn't much better.

"I love football. I don't know why," he said, slow and painstaking. "I can start with what I don't like and get that out of the way."

"Okay."

"I don't like it when I'm hit and a mob suffocates me. And I don't like the name-calling. Guys from the other team calling us bitches when we're in formation."

"Really?"

"But even our own guys do that to each other during practices. Everyone's a bitch. They say they're trying to toughen us up, but I think they like it."

This was going to take a long time. All questions—even simple ones—engulfed him. I snuggled into his side, hoping I wouldn't fall asleep. I really did want to listen, but the warmth, the coziness, the rumbling of his voice in his chest, all made me drowsy. I felt satisfied and content, growing sleepy in someone's arms.

"I don't have much patience for guys who don't pay attention and screw things up for us. Our team does okay, but considering we're not in the Suburban League, which is much bigger and more competitive, we should be doing great. We should be at the top."

"Oh, yeah?"

"Coach Pisetti trusts me, probably because I'm one of the few people on the team to do what I'm told. Some of these guys think it's a race. They just want the ball so they can score. I don't understand what's so hard about playing your position when it's time to do it. If it weren't for the size of some of our guys, or their speed, our team would be in chaos."

"Sophia Baldini did that in *Once Upon a Mattress* in seventh grade," I said. "I helped make the sets. On opening night she started playing to the audience, making faces and making up lines and doing shout-outs to her friends. People were laughing, but she made a big mess. I thought the director was going to faint."

"Yes, that's it," he said. "You rehearse something and then someone tries to steal the show." He breathed in deep, his huge chest expanding. "Maybe things will be different this fall. Every year a team has a different makeup. But we're losing some talent, some seniors. And some of this year's juniors aren't necessarily team players."

"Let me guess," I said.

"Yes, Mr. Samson. Not sportsmanlike. He's always lecturing us like he's Mr. Pisetti's assistant, then breaking his own rules. And the way he talks to some players. Do you know Fred Conrad?"

Fred Conrad was Amy Conrad's older brother, a year ahead of us. He was a big, strong guy, very athletic, but also an outsider. Very odd, and kind of odd-looking, too.

"He really tried. He wasn't great, but he tried. He was an okay player, just not fast. And Boz always called him Roadrunner because Fred was notoriously slow on laps and lagged behind everyone else. I don't see what difference that makes, but sometimes he was so slow that Mr. Pisetti would make us run another lap because he had taken so long. It was a team joke, but it shouldn't have been. We should have been encouraging him for trying. I wonder why he even stuck with it."

"Maybe he was like you—he loved the game."

"When you think about it," he said, as if he hadn't heard me, "it's pretty arrogant to make fun of someone else, like you're going to the pros yourself."

"So what do you like about it?" I asked, afraid I might lose my battle with sleep.

"The order. Everything makes sense—if you play as a team and not as an individual. And the greatest thing in the world is your players being exactly where they're supposed to be during a play."

His breathing got a little deeper, and I thought he might fall asleep himself. But he wasn't done with my question.

"You know, there's something magical about it, at the end of the season when it gets dark early but practice is still three to six, daylight or not. Running laps in the snow. My hands cracking and bleeding from the cold. Practice gets over in the pitch blackness, and by the time Mr. Pisetti blows the whistle, we're almost icicles."

"And you like that?"

"Well, it feels good in a way, like discipline making me stronger and able to handle things. Also there's a long, hot shower to come. Nothing feels so good."

"Nothing?" I asked.

He looked at me, unsure.

"I mean," I said, "considering you've spent the last hour with me."

"Oh, oh," he said, "now I understand." He turned on his side, looked at me with those eyes. "I meant, nothing feels so good when you're that cold and dirty. I wouldn't even think of putting my arms around you then."

His literalness made me smile. "You know how to make a girl feel special," I said.

"I understand now. No, you see, the two have nothing in common ...."

I put my finger up to his lips.

"Cas, you are so sweet. I mean it." Then, following a pulse of insecurity, I said, "I don't know how I'm going to keep those girls off you next season." This was a risk, since it assumed we would still be together by then.

"What girls?"

"Cheerleaders."

"I wish they would ride on a different bus for away games," he said. "It's crazy. I don't know how you're supposed to play after you've used up all your energy during the trip."

I did not want to know what kind of energy was used up on the bus. Even though they were only day trips, his away games would be taking him from me next fall. Already I was a possessive girlfriend.

Caspar wasn't done intoning.

"I don't really approve of the things they do, the cheerleaders," he said, lying on his back and looking at the ceiling. "They bake stuff—brownies, cookies—and leave them in guys' lockers. Candy. Inspirational notes. Clean out their lockers for them. Decorate them."

"Did anyone ever bake you brownies and leave them in your locker?" I asked, feeling slightly cold.

"A few times it's happened."

I couldn't stop myself. "Who?"

"The last thing I remember is a paper plate with fudge brownies, with those candy decorations on top. From Sandy Willis."

I wondered if he could feel my heartbeat change. Sandy had been a Holy Redeemer girl like me, chubby back then. Now she was beautiful and willowy. She had done nothing to harm me, but I wanted her parents to get jobs far, far away.

"It seems to me that stuff has nothing to do with the sport."

He was right. But still I wanted to decorate his locker for him, fill it with brownies, show the world who my man was. Until Pan caught me.

"I'm glad you feel that way," I said despite myself.

"That's one of the things I like about you. You're a very independent girl, aren't you?" He pretended to wrestle, which ended with me pinned underneath him. This was as playful as he'd ever been.

But Caspar was not Pan, so when I said, "Let me go, you brute," he rolled off and sat up.

"Oh my gosh, I'm sorry. Did I hurt you?"

"Cas," I said, fully awake now and pulling him back, "I was kidding. Kidding."

"I don't always understand your sense of humor," he said.

"I know. I'm sorry. I like to joke around. When I feel really comfortable with someone."

"I see. Well, that's good, then. I like that. As long as you're not going to call the police." He kind of grinned.

"Promise."

I realized then that I really knew so little about him and I was impatient to know everything. "Can I ask you something else, Cas?" I asked.

"Sure," he said.

"Was your story for school about your own family? You told me you had two older brothers, but that's all I know. I just wondered."

He didn't say anything. His big chest moved up and down, reliable, impressive. Maybe I had tweaked a nerve and we were in for our first unpleasant scene. If so, I would apologize and drop it.

Caspar, however, was contemplating, not angry. Finally, he said, "They were much, much worse than that in real life. I haven't heard from them since I was eleven. I'm not even sure my parents know where they are or what they're doing."

He breathed a little faster.

"Mom and Dad had gone out for the evening. This was in our old house. Clinton and Joe came over because their stepdad had kicked them out again. They were a lot older. I can't remember much, but my parents came home and found the babysitter screaming and dragging me out of the house. They were fighting with knives. I guess they couldn't get along with anybody, not even each other. Twins."

"I didn't know they were twins."

"Police intervention, and court, and detention, and all that stuff. I think my mom banned them from our house after that. It makes sense, but then they were gone for good. They might be in jail for all I know."

His house was so neat and quiet, I couldn't picture it ever having been a violent circus.

"But the strangest thing is, Nia, I miss them. They're in their twenties now, and I barely know them."

I ran my hand up and down his arm. Everything he told me about himself made me surer I wanted to be his girlfriend for keeps. "I'm sorry," I said. "Has anyone told them about your dad's, you know, problems?"

He turned. "I don't know. I haven't asked. They're my brothers, but somehow I don't feel it's my place to. Isn't that strange?"

"No, not really."

"But you, you are the best thing in my life. You're so normal. Your family is so normal, from what I can tell."

He didn't know my parents very well and he hadn't heard Paolo. But I didn't argue. In the quiet that followed, I realized that a major evolution had taken place so fast in my life. I had wanted a boyfriend since I could remember. Now I actually had one, without much effort and with only minimal praying. The girl who was convinced she'd never find a guy had found a great one. I felt serene, peaceful, as if the air around us insisted on it. I had to be at work in an hour, but I let myself fall asleep in that tranquility.

Chapter 20

Once I was dating Caspar, I noticed that Pan barely mentioned him. He didn't change the subject when I brought him up, or get angry or anything like that. He just didn't engage.

Other things I didn't notice right away. Pan called me less often. He had been calling me three or four times a day, which I had taken for granted. Now it was once a day, usually at night. He also had stopped assuming I had free time. First it was weekends, but then it was weekdays, too. He still came to the pharmacy, but less often, and it took me a few weeks to realize that I hadn't been to his house and he hadn't been to mine in a week or so. Maybe it was something of a relief that he didn't insist on so much of my time. I didn't argue with this convenience. In school we still ate lunch at our table—just the two of us—and spent almost all our rare minutes of free time together.

While my relationship with Caspar was going along nicely, as if we had been together for years instead of weeks, things were not going so well for him at home. His dad's condition was not improving. He had survived the surgery, but he was staying in the hospital a lot longer than heart patients normally did. When he wasn't visiting the hospital, Caspar was alone at his house. I did meet his aunt and his mom once, in passing. They were polite but in a rush. His mom was thin and wiry with a short, efficient hairdo, nothing like Caspar. She was clipped and businesslike with me, but complimentary.

"Caspar says such nice things about you," she said with a firm handshake. "I'm pleased he has a good friend."

Finally, his dad came home. But not only didn't I meet him, I didn't see his mom or aunt again. Caspar said it was fine that we hung out, as long as we stayed in the basement, which had its own outside entrance. The cellar was practically an apartment by itself, with a half bathroom, a bar, and the kitchenette. And the movies were making me feel right at home, too. Caspar would spend quite a bit of time explaining two or three that he had set aside as possibilities for the evening. I figured out that it was better to be decisive, tell him which one sounded best even if I didn't have a solid opinion, or else the selection process would go on past my curfew. I had never heard of any of them, and I was surprised at how much I liked some of those obscure stories.

Without discussing it, we had been having our private time first, because if we got started during the film, we wouldn't see the end of it. I couldn't let myself think about how the happiest time of my life was happening two floors below where Caspar's dad was fighting for his. Caspar didn't tell me a lot about what was going on above, only that the surgery had not been a cure.

By early May the strange and fragile cafeteria arrangement started swaying. One day Pan caught me making eye contact across the room. I don't remember now what he and I were talking about, but he seemed to go into a trance. He barely talked the rest of lunch. It wasn't like he was mad, more like he had been hypnotized.

"Don't be like that," I said, trying to be funny. "You are so possessive." But I could hear the falseness in my tone, and he would not banter.

The next day Pan was late for lunch. He had an extra advanced math class twice a week, so we didn't walk to the cafeteria together those days. I sat at our table and waited, eating listlessly, growing more uncomfortable.

"It's stupid for us not to sit at the same table," Caspar said, appearing in front of me with his tray.

I looked up as if he were a stranger. "I guess ...." He sat down right next to me, which felt somehow more intimate than when we were lying next to each other. Then he kissed my lips in front of all those people. I was rigid.

"I know James is shy," Caspar said. "But I really would like to get to know him. He's your best friend."

I stopped my robotic eating and put my hand on his. "That's really nice of you, Cas."

"We haven't talked about this, but I've been assuming you'll want to go to the prom with me. Unless you have other plans."

I tried to remember how serious Pan and I had been about the prom. I wanted to go with Caspar, a genuine date that wasn't a protest or a consolation.

I laughed like I had just heard something silly.

"I would love to," I said. "But I'm not much for that kind of thing."

"Oh," he said, looking stung and putting his sandwich to his mouth. "Oh." He took a halfhearted bite.

"I don't know where James is today," I said.

"He's sitting over there," Caspar said. "I just noticed him come in."

I turned around. Pan sat at a table by himself, his tall body arched over his food. He didn't look sad or lonely, more bored and indifferent, like a businessman out for dinner alone. He looked over and I saw nothing but effort in his smile. In just those few seconds I had tipped the two men in my life overboard.

The bell rang, and they were both gone.

~

"Nia, I'm so glad to see you," Kevin said, giving me a long hug. I had not called in advance, just stopped in. Seeing Pan alone at lunch had practically driven me here. "We've missed you. I hear your boyfriend is very nice. Honey, I think that's great."

"Yeah," I said.

"James is a little blue that you're not coming around so much. I offered to be his new best friend, but somehow he didn't think much of the offer." He laughed. "What he needs is a nice boy for himself. He just can't seem to settle on any one for too long. Of course, we move around like gypsies, which doesn't help. Anyway, tell me about your guy."

I couldn't remember Caspar at that moment. I didn't know what he looked like or where he lived or any traits that made him human. He was only a shape in my mind.

"He plays football," said Kevin. "That much I know."

"Fullback," I said, hoping I was remembering right. "He's a big guy, but fast."

"Might as well be a goalie for all I know about sports," he said. "Good for you, though. Young love. Nothing like it."

"Yeah," Pan said, walking in.

"Well, I'll leave you kids alone. Nice to see you again, honey."

"Nice to see you too, Kevin," I said, sounding a bit weary.

The atmosphere was heavy when we got to Pan's room,

though nothing he said or did should have made me feel that way. We watched some video clips on his laptop. But we didn't add any commentary.

"Want something to eat?" he asked after a long half hour went by. Usually he didn't ask, just took me down and fed me.

"Uh, I'd like to. But I'd better go home and relieve my mom for a while before I go to work."

"How is my boy Paolo?"

"The same. You know, he has his good days and his bad days." I was about to say, "He misses you," but that was a kind of admission, and the room felt too small for it.

I could not break this awkwardness. "Call me tonight at the store," I said. "Or come by. Definitely come by."

"Okay. Let me walk you out. I'm not going to make you go by Gram without a bodyguard."

It didn't help that he was with me, because the old woman demanded to know why I was late delivering the paper. "You're getting a little sloppy with your work there, mister," she said.

"See ya," I said, and Pan closed the door. I tried to convince myself it was his grandmother being there that kept him from saying good-bye.

Caspar called me that night at work. I tried to keep my mind on the conversation.

"Is there something the matter?" he finally asked. "Was it the prom thing?"

He was so good that I almost laughed. It was the first unwound moment I'd had that day.

"No, no," I said. "It's not you at all. I'm upset about a friend."

"James."

I didn't answer at first, and I was sure he could tell that

meant yes.

"Yeah, a small misunderstanding."

"Is that why he was sitting alone?"

"Something like that."

"He seems hard to predict."

"He's going through a hard time right now."

"I'm very sorry to hear that. I hope it's not more of people knocking him around."

"Not lately, no."

"I really think he should talk to the vice principal. If he doesn't get anywhere with her, maybe he should think about a lawyer."

Evidently, I could fall and fall in love with Caspar and never hit bottom. I wanted to see him tonight, but I couldn't. I had to call Pan and get out of the freezer.

"I'll miss you," Caspar said. "Call me tomorrow. And if you think it's appropriate, tell James I hope he's doing okay."

"I will."

"Good night, Nia. I love you."

To think I would have considered a little fooling around with Ted Karsinski in ninth grade if he would have taken me to a stupid dance. I was glad circumstances had made me wait two and a half years for a decent guy. But for now, I had to get another guy back.

I called Pan from the card aisle where I was sorting. "Pan," I said when he answered.

"Hi."

"I'm at work. I had to talk to you. Look, I'm not very good at this kind of thing, but you're my best friend and I want you to stay my best friend, and I don't want us to be this way. It's my fault, I know."

I waited.

"I'm sorry I've been spending so much time with Caspar."

"You think he's prettier?"

"No one is prettier."

"I know that, silly girl."

"Why didn't you sit with me today?"

"You mean with us."

"Okay, but I was waiting for you specifically. I was there by myself and feeling self-conscious. I didn't know if you were coming."

"It's fine. I don't mind. He is your boyfriend, after all."

"He is, but he only needs one chair. I can't believe you were by yourself."

"I didn't want to intrude. I figured you wanted some time together. "

"You weren't, you know, jealous or mad?"

"No. Would you be jealous if I had a boyfriend?"

"Sure I would," I said. "But I wouldn't tell you. That's what friends do for each other."

"Lie?"

"Sometimes."

"Listen, Caspar came over to my table—our table—without asking."

"He doesn't have to ask, Nia. It makes sense he wouldn't want you to sit by yourself."

"But you didn't have to sit alone."

"That's the only other person I know at school. Me."

"He thinks you don't like him. I mean, it's okay if you don't, but ...."

"He does? I never said a word."

"That might be why."

"He's kind of an okay guy. Not so bad."

"Not so bad."

"I'm not talking about in bed."

"Neither am I."

"I knew it," he said. "He's terrible in bed."

"I hate you."

"Does that mean everything's back to normal, Nia Santa Maria, that you hate me again?"

"I think it does. For the record, we have been on his bed but not in it."

"That is restraint. Never had any, myself."

"I felt so weird at your house this afternoon. I don't ever want it to be like that again."

"Then I want you to come over more often."

"I will. And please sit with me. Caspar wanted to get to know you. He said so."

"Maybe I'll let him sit with us from now on," he said. "Let me bring this to the Central Council. How many chairs did you say he requires?"

"Just one."

"Okay, then enough about him. Any other gossip tonight?"

"There's one more thing. He asked me to the prom."

"What? That's not one more thing. That's everything."

"And I said no."

"Don't you usually flit off to your guidance counselor in times like that?"

"Not this time. I told him no."

"Did you tell him you already had a date?"

"Not exactly."

"What did you tell him?"

"I just ... said it wasn't my thing."

"So what's he going to think when you show up with me?"

"I hadn't thought about it. Maybe we shouldn't go either. Neither of us really wants to."

"I do want to. To show you off."

A few seconds went by. He sighed, then said, "Go with Caspar. Seriously."

"No, I said no, and that's it. I'm not even going to think about it. His dad is still sick and not getting any better, from what I can tell. I don't want to jerk him around. He looked like a scolded puppy today when I turned him down."

"Well, all right. I guess I forgives ya for all your faults. All your grievous faults. But this discussion will be continued."

"Nia, customers!" Tammie shouted from across the store.

"Got to go. Loves ya."

"Is Tammie in full spasm again?"

"Full."

"Tell her no one names their kids Tammie anymore."

I hung up, breathing in relief, and ran back to the register to help one of our sweet customers who would have a handful of change to pay for a bottle of lotion.

Chapter 21

My mom had told me, in one of her less frazzled moments, that sometimes everything just seems to be working out. "There have been a few of them, these times," she said, "since I started realizing they existed."

"That's nice to hear, Mom," I said. This was the kind of talk I liked from her—optimism, instead of remorse about her life choices. Or sex advice.

"Just before I got saddled with your brother was one of them."

Maybe she wasn't so optimistic. But then she saved it: "You and Teo were pretty much independent, and I was going back to school to do something with my life. Your dad's business was humping along at the time. All of a sudden I realized things were aligned, all working the way I wanted them to."

"Then Paolo," I said.

"The whole thing with Paolo ... well, I don't feel like that destroys my theory. Things were working out, and I don't believe they were destined to get gnarled up." She sucked her teeth. "But having everything running parallel is temporary.

So you need to enjoy it when things are good."

I was going through just such a period. If I ignored all the things that were unchangeably wrong—money problems, Caspar's dad's health—things were gliding in unison as if that were the natural way. I had Pan, I had Caspar, my grades were good, and my job was safe for the time being. The owner had told Tammie that two new residences might be opening downtown, and like the others, they would have their prescription accounts with us.

Lunchtime was still awkward. Caspar was now part of our table, and the conversation was almost nonexistent. At first our discomfort was like a fourth person sitting with us. But Caspar's presence made me feel secure. No one had ever bothered Pan in the broadness of the cafeteria lights, and having a giant football player on our team made it unlikely that anyone would. Maybe the unspoken protection would keep Pan from getting shoved into another locker. I decided to lean back into Mom's theory of parallelism.

But that didn't mean no one was watching.

Pan's locker was across the hall from Caspar's, down a few yards. Our routine now was that at the end of the day, Pan would wait by his locker for me to say good-bye to Caspar before he went to track practice. Pan stood with his back straight against the row, backpack in front of him. I ignored him because if I didn't, he would point to his expensive watch to indicate it was time to get walking.

After school one day Caspar and I were talking a little when I heard Samsonite say, exaggerating every idiotic word, "Hey, still eating a dick?" I turned fast, expecting Pan to be slapped or pushed or something, but Samsonite did his rooster walk toward us. Then he stopped at Caspar's locker.

"Yo, it's the Cas-man. Where you been at?" He acted like they hadn't seen each other in years. "Why don't you eat with us no more, Cas-man?"

"I don't know," Caspar said, starting to pack his bag.

Samsonite bounced on his feet. "Why'd you ditch us? Sittin' there with your two sisters."

I don't know what Caspar reminded me of then—a robot maybe. He stood straight and turned, and his hands jetted out faster than I'd ever seen him do anything. He grabbed Samsonite by the shirt and pushed him against the lockers, holding him there.

"Don't say anything about my girlfriend," he said, then lifted Samsonite just high enough so their eyes were even.

"Okay, okay," Samsonite said, trying to laugh. "It's cool. We're cool. I mean it."

Caspar slammed him once against the locker, then dropped him. He went back to packing, as if he'd already forgotten his rage. Samsonite kept forcing a dry, unanimated laugh. He even turned to me and said, "You know I'm just fooling around. You're cool and all." Then he said, "Caspar Phillips, man. See ya."

When Caspar didn't look back at him, Samsonite turned, nodding his head as if things were going as planned, and started walking away.

"See ya," he called. Caspar shut his locker hard. He looked at me, put his arms around my waist, and kissed me good-bye.

He didn't mention the incident, so I didn't.

"He was pretty good," Pan said on our way home. "He's impassive mostly, then suddenly a beast. I like it."

"Yeah," I said.

"I'm glad he's on my side. Sort of."

There was more to say, but neither of us did.

~

A couple days after that scene, Pan said something that

actually made Caspar laugh. A laugh from him was something you noticed, deep and rumbling and commanding. And there was a slight delay between the cause and the effect. The information had to travel many serious miles to get to his funny bone.

We were at a lull in conversation, which was not unusual, when we heard Samsonite's very loud response to something at his table, followed by raucous laughter. Pan shook his head.

"Too much sugar," I said.

"Too much breast milk," said Pan.

Caspar stopped eating, as if to examine the hypothesis. Then his face went from its usual tight concentration to a bursting laugh. It was deep enough to be an entire baritone section.

Pan looked at him with a pleased curiosity.

At the end of his laugh, Caspar nodded to Pan, who, I believe, actually blushed before he looked away.

I took a bite of the eggplant parm sandwich my mom had made, the slices all parallel. It was, like this moment, delicious.

Chapter 22

I didn't have the money to go to Cape Cod for Memorial Day weekend. I didn't have the money to go anywhere, not even Triangle or Root. Also, if I wasn't around, who would help Mom with Paolo? What about the pharmacy? How could I be sure there would be a job waiting for me when I got back? I didn't get vacation days or sick time. Tammie took them, but she would disapprove of me missing a shift. No doubt I would hear about the sacrifices she'd had to make in my absence.

Pan didn't want to hear it.

"All you need is some spending money," he said. "And if you don't have that, I have it for you. I let you out of the prom thing, but I have my limits."

I told Mom and Dad I would have my own room on the Cape, which might have been true for all I knew at the time. I didn't bother to update them when the final arrangements were made and I was going to be staying in the same suite with Pan. Dad couldn't possibly be worried that Pan posed a danger, since that would undermine his prejudices. And Mom trusted Pan like a son. Also, they'd both made cryptic remarks about Caspar never coming to our house. They had only met him that once for a few seconds, then seen him with his tongue in my mouth after. And they probably suspected that he was my first love, so to speak. So surely they were glad I was getting away from him and all those temptations that they didn't know for sure I had given in to.

Caspar didn't exactly twitch with excitement when I told him I was going away with Pan's family for the long weekend, but he studied it, sat with it for a while, then told me that I should have fun.

Pan's parents were happy he had someone to keep him company. I enjoyed the thought of spending time with Kevin, but I was a little concerned about Ada. However, I forgot all about being nervous when we got to Chatham and I was introduced to the concept of luxury.

The Cranberry Inn was a huge Victorian house with turrets and massive windows that sat right on the beach. It was a new building, and Pan's mom informed me that this architecture was not historically correct for beachfront property.

I didn't care if it was. A porch ran all the way along the back, facing the ocean. The main room of our suite had a long cream couch across from a landscape TV, a couple of leather armchairs, a coffee table, and a small desk. Our bedrooms were not a lot bigger than the over-pillowed double beds that filled them. I could get spoiled by such extravagance, and for the first time I regretted being poor, truly regretted it, rather than just being burdened by it.

I couldn't bring myself to think about what this must have cost or that I was spending Pan's parents' money, even though they insisted on it.

"We have to rent a room for James anyway," Kevin had said. "You're not costing us a dime."

The view was worth every trace of guilt: Outside the sliding glass doors was the ocean. I was torn between staying inside to soak in the luxury and getting out in that sand and those waves. I watched the sea sending waves in and pulling them back and never lost interest. Sitting near the water, close enough for my feet to get tickled by the frigid surf without a full assault, I could picture living somewhere else besides Mungers Mills, being perfectly content with a career that involved watching waves.

On our first day at the beach, Pan and I were like ten-year-olds. Kevin had put together a picnic basket of drinks and packaged snacks for us. We played in the frigid waves until we lost feeling in our limbs. The sand was warm though, and afterward I fell asleep on that grainy mattress.

Pan wanted authentic beach junk food, so we waited in a long line at a white, open-air shack. When we got our mammoth soft pretzels, some guy who was about 80 asked Pan if he wanted some decent food. His sentences kept ending with things like "a young fella like you."

"You shouldn't eat junk food, a young fella like you."

Then, as if there were no police in all of Massachusetts, he told Pan to reach into his pocket and fish out some money. "My hands are full," was his excuse. They were, since he was carrying a cardboard tray of sodas. But it was a sorry excuse.

"Mine, too," Pan said, waving with his free hand as we walked off.

"Oh, gross," I said. "Can you believe that?"

"Right in public this wrinkleton is trying to pick me up. He's probably got a wife, too. A thirsty one."

"Should we tell your mom?"

"Sure. You know how level she is."

"She ought to know."

"She chips a nail and she's planning a class-action suit. Besides, he didn't follow me or try to kidnap me or anything. Maybe he thought I was older."

"You're still a hundred years younger than him."

"Kind of flattering, don't you think?"

"Please be careful. Don't go off with any old men. They'll get you in an isolated spot and you'll never be seen again."

"Until the podcast comes out."

"Don't even joke about it."

"I'll be fine, especially if you're there to protect me."

"I will be. But you might have to wear a less revealing bathing suit for me to have any luck."

Pan and I were mostly on our own. The only thing his parents insisted on was dinner together, and they took us to restaurants where the prices made me blanch. I had cashed and kept all of my last paycheck instead of giving some to Mom. She had insisted. She even tried to slip me some more money, but I wouldn't take it. I had a plan that when the bill came at the end of each meal, I would pull out some cash to pay my own share. When the money ran out—which would be very, very soon at these rates—I would say I wasn't hungry, and hit up vending machines. But Pan's parents didn't hear me when I offered. I ordered the cheapest things at first, sometimes an appetizer instead of an entree, though nothing was cheap. As early as Friday night Pan caught on and changed my order. When I asked for a hamburger, he said, "You love shrimp. Shrimp grow on trees here at the shore."

"I'm in the mood for a burger," I said, not even convincing myself. "The sea air makes me hungry."

"You're having the shrimp. You're not in Mungers-burger anymore."

So I had the shrimp, another exhilaration. My parents

were not even eating together, never mind having shrimp in a pricey restaurant. Dad would be working late, Mom would catch something between Paolo's intermittent shrieking. Later they would watch TV in our living room with the aging wallpaper. I was sitting here eating like royalty before going back to my suite. I reasoned that this was the kind of life Mom wanted for me. Someday I'd find a way to bring her here and live this life, for at least a weekend.

None of the indulgence was wasted, because I ate everything put in front of me. Pan wanted dessert, but I refused because the desserts started at twelve dollars. He would have to force-feed me before I let him pay that. So of course he ordered one for each of us. Mine was a chocolate tart with raspberries, which were never in season in Mungers Mills. Kevin paid what must have been a mammoth bill without even blinking.

On Saturday night when we were done eating, Kevin asked us, "So what are you two beach bums going to do this evening? Any plans with the local kids?"

"We're gonna hang out at the surf shop with Dale and Missy," Pan said. "They're swell."

Kevin smiled, tilted his head a little. "Our James," he said. "Light of our lives."

"Answer the question, James," Ada said. "Or I'll send you home to Grandma."

"Nothing much," I said. "We're going to walk through town."

"Be careful," Kevin said. "And if you go to the beach again tomorrow, those July fish can take you by surprise. Remember how you used to call them 'July fish,' James? I kept telling him jellyfish come in August!"

"No, Kev, because it didn't happen."

"Did so."

"Did not. You made it up. All your stories are manufactured in China."

Kevin looked at me. "He used to be such a sweet little boy, Nia."

"So now I'm sour?"

"Heavens no," Kevin said, and winked at me. "Of course, there was the time when I tried to walk him to school and we passed this nice old woman—"

"Kevin," Pan warned.

"Enough male bonding," Ada said. "Let's go. I want to hit that hot tub before too many people get the same idea."

The streets in town were lined with pedestrians, T-shirt stores, and taffy shops. Pan wasn't exactly parting the waters as he walked through the crowds, but I started taking note after the fifth or sixth inappropriate double take. I thought it might have been about me being with such a hot boy until I realized that most of the gawkers were male and no one was looking at me at all. Men of all ages checked out my golden-headed friend. Young guys with dress shorts and perfect hair. Other men, older, some with what appeared to be their wives and children. Maybe some girls turned, too, but I was fascinated by the consistent male attention. And for some reason it made me lonesome for Caspar.

"I need to get a T-shirt for Paolo," I said, turning into a shop. This was half the truth, as I also wanted one for Caspar.

"Hi," Pan said to a kid folding a pile of loose tees whose name tag said CHRIS. He looked to be our age, maybe a little older, with white, white skin behind a beard shadow. The sleeves on his shirt could barely restrain his toned arms.

"How may I help you?" he asked Pan. He sounded so eager I thought he might kiss Pan hello.

"Need a shirt for my friend's baby brother," Pan said,

nodding my way. Chris, with his thin, trimmed black hair, smiled at me a second.

"Where are the toddlers' clothes?" I asked, but they had both already forgotten me. I was embarrassed, but also interested in how the pickup thing was done. I could never do it myself, not with a complete stranger. I wandered away, leaving Pan to his hyperattentive salesboy.

I felt awkward about spending money on souvenirs when Pan's parents were giving me a free vacation. But it was my first experience at buying something for a boyfriend. Caspar would only wear T-shirts if they didn't have huge logos or graphics on them. I found one, a deep blue with small, gold lettering. Then I found another, black lettering on white with a minute seashell design near the words. I found an all-black one for Pan that I was sure would set off his blond hair, and a toddler-size one for Paolo that would look the way everything looked on him.

It shouldn't have mattered, but it turned out that Chris was the only cashier. So when I sneaked over to what seemed to be a secondary checkout counter, he bounced over, somewhat flushed, smile wide and almost crazed. Stretched any farther, his face would crack. Pan came, too, but like a schoolmaster approaching with a cane. He took one of the giant shirts from me.

"A tent for Paolo."

"Pan."

"Pan?" Chris asked.

"Short for Pansy," Pan said, and turned back to me. Chris looked startled.

"Two tents for Paolo."

"They're for Caspar," I said, though I could have claimed they were nightgowns for my mom. "Which you know."

"Casper?" Chris asked, recovered. Then, like he was

already part of the family, he added, "Casper the Friendly Ghost?"

"My boyfriend," I said.

"So you two aren't together?" Chris continued with that loony smile.

"Now you're annoying me," Pan said to him. He turned back to me. "Pay for them. Let's get going."

Chris's smile snapped shut and his face went red. He bagged my shirts as if he didn't know what he was doing. Pan was already outside on the walk. Chris handed me the bag.

"Have a really great night," he said, even though his was clearly ruined.

Outside, Pan walked a little too fast for me. I could feel the thrill of the seashore slipping down a sewer grate.

"What's wrong?" I called, trying to keep up and talk at the same time.

"Nothing. Let's go back to the room."

"Okay, but why are you so mad? I just wanted souvenirs. Is it because your parents are paying? I can pay them back."

He stopped, turned to me. "Why do you have to rub it in my face?"

Every nerve in my body jammed in my throat. He had never sounded so mean before.

"Rub what in your face?"

"You said you were getting one for Paolo."

"I did."

"Where is it?"

"It's in the bag with the rest of them."

"They're for what's-his-name."

"Two of them are. One's for you. What's the crime? Like I said, if it's the money —"

"I don't care about money. Let's go."

We made our way, not talking, through the crowded streets. We walked toward the end of the commercial section. By then my bewilderment was turning to anger. I had to say something before we were back at the inn.

It came out sharper than I expected.

"Pan, what is your problem? All of a sudden I'm evil because I buy something for my boyfriend? While you're cruising another guy?"

"I wasn't cruising."

"Oh, please. You weren't exchanging recipes. I may be a small-town girl but I'm not a complete idiot."

Finally, he slowed down. "He was cute, wasn't he, my cashier boy?"

"No diversions. You were hitting on each other, and then you remembered I was there, and you threw your fit. And those are the facts."

"It wasn't a fit. Just a tiny outburst."

"You hurt that guy's feelings."

"Really?"

"Yeah, really. Didn't you see how his face fell when you stopped paying attention to him and started on me?"

"Well, no."

"I think you should go back and apologize. He liked you, and you were mean to him so you could be mean to me."

"Was I mean?"

"Oh, my God, are you absent today? So I bought Caspar a present."

"Two."

"Two. I'm here with you, aren't I? Why can't we have a good time?"

"Maybe you want to go home."

"I'm not saying anything until you grow up."

He stopped walking, turned, and put his hands on my

shoulders.

"Nia, I loves ya awful. Maybe I'm worried."

"No need to be. I'm still your best friend."

"I don't want to share. Not this weekend. This is my time with you, not his."

My nerves unwound a bit.

"I'm a smart girl," I said. "Like I told you before, I can have two people in my life." I understood clearly at that moment how hard that was turning out to be, but I was determined more than ever to make it true.

"I don't want to lose you," he said. It wasn't simpering or pathetic, just plain and painful honesty.

"You won't, dummy."

"Promise?"

"Promise."

"Okay, but you promised to go to the prom with me."

"I'm not going at all. I told him no, and that was the end of it. You and Caspar can go together."

"Couldn't you get really tiny so I could carry you around in my pocket forever?"

"Go patch things up with Chris."

"Chris? Oh, okay, Chris."

"And while you're doing that, I am going to call Caspar, without acting like a secret agent or something."

"Hug first," he said. I pulled him close, and I could smell the sea air on him.

Chapter 23

Caspar's dad was like a character in a play who's talked about but never appears on stage. So when Mom called me at the inn Sunday night to tell me he had died, it wasn't quite real. In our phone conversation the evening before, Caspar hadn't mentioned his dad—he rarely did—so I assumed things hadn't gotten worse. But Mom said that according to the Sunday death notices in the local paper, Mr. Phillips had been "stricken at home" Saturday night.

I called Caspar, but straight to voicemail.

I couldn't concentrate on anything else. Pan sensed my disorientation, and he held my hand on the drive home from the Cape the next day in the agonizing holiday traffic. He was a crutch for me during my weird mourning.

"You realize," he said when we finally got close to home late that night, "that you have to go to the prom with him."

"That is so not now," I said.

"It isn't, I know. But you will have to go."

"He's not going to want to do anything," I said. Pan patted my hand.

~

I phoned again when I was in my room that night, and still no answer. Then I tried his home number, even though his family would surely be deluged with calls. Someone with a husky voice told me brusquely that she would pass my message on to him. I didn't call again. When I told Pan how awful it was going to be waiting to hear from Caspar, he said, "You'll be able to talk to him at the service, if there is one."

"I guess. I don't like that sort of thing, though."

"Neither do I, but you don't have a choice. He's going to want you there."

"I know. I just don't like dead bodies. Especially when I never met them alive."

"It is a strange way to get acquainted."

"I haven't actually been to a wake since my Great-aunt Carmeta."

"What about poor Great-aunt Carmeta?"

"They made her look like—I don't know what. They had her hair all big and poofy, and red like you've never seen. A full-length, scary evening gown that was also red. And tons of makeup. It was like one of those glamour photos, only with a dead person."

"Caspar's father will not look like an elderly chorus girl, I promise," he said. "And it might be just a memorial service. I'll go with you, either way."

"You're a good friend," I said.

"The best," he said.

~

Mom had been invited to an open house for "nontraditional students" at the community college. She was determined to get to school this coming fall. That would have been great news except it meant Paolo was going with us to the calling hours for Caspar's dad. Dad was not able to leave work early. There were no babysitters to call on short notice, especially with Paolo's reputation.

I didn't have a dress to wear. It had been so long since I'd worn anything but jeans that I wasn't ready for a formal event. I tried on an old pair of black wool pants that had been hanging in my closet for years, but they looked awful on me. None of my blouses hung right. There was also an old pair of cords that were worse than jeans. I couldn't borrow Mom's clothes because we had different bodies. I settled for a black button-down blouse and the least-worn jeans I had.

This was going to be awful. And it had started to sprinkle.

Pan looked like a movie star in his black suit and tie. He needed to sit with Paolo in the backseat, so I drove his mom's car. I had to park far away because the funeral home lot was full and there were lines of cars on the streets.

As long as Paolo had Pan's hair to pull, he could be taken from the car seat without making a sound. Pan grimaced but didn't stop him. We were walking past the pharmacy when Paolo realized it was raining and began whining. I tried to hold an umbrella over the two of them, getting wet myself.

"I'll take the baby and stay in the vestibule, and you go in and scope things out," Pan said. "He's going to be glad to see you." Paolo pulled his hair. "Go on, before I'm bald."

It was pouring now, and my brother was as angry as the sky. We had to get inside.

"No," Paolo said like a baby drill sergeant as we walked in. "No no no."

A streak of lightning followed by a thunderclap sent us into a trot. Paolo went silent so fast that I thought he had been struck. Then he let me know he was as hearty as ever by starting to shout an octave higher. He wriggled fiercely in Pan's arms, indifferent to his best friend now.

"Maybe we should take him to the hospital," Pan said.

"No, he's okay," I said. "His color is good. We've been through this many times. Why don't you take him to—?" The attention in the vestibule had all turned to us. "I don't know what to do."

A somber, official-looking man came tapping down the stairs toward us.

"I can take you to a private lounge," he said. Paolo shrieked at him. The man leaned toward my left ear. "We really need to consider the family."

"Give me that," Pan said, taking the umbrella from me. He looked at the man. "If we get hit by lightning, we'll be in the right place." Then he opened the umbrella and said, "Oh no, bad luck," and forced it out the door the man earnestly held open for them. "Nia," he called, "go on. I'll wait for you." The man pulled the door tight. Thunder smacked like a plane exploding over the building.

I forced my way up the stairs and into the main room. I was drenched, and my hair must have looked like it had been vacuumed. The place was crowded, and everyone was taller than me. I couldn't even tell which direction I was going as I pushed through. It wasn't until I saw the big glass window that I got my bearings. And it was when I remembered that Bianchini Funeral Home had a spooky setup where you viewed the body through a window into this cave-like room set off from the rest of the parlor.

I saw Caspar standing next to his mom. When I was in front of him, I realized they were receiving a long line of people—including Samsonite and Patrick Torno and other football buddies—which I had managed to butt to the front of. I heard, "Wait your turn," which could have been from any of them.

"Nia."

"Casket," I said. "Caspar, I mean. I have to go. Paolo—my

baby brother—is with me. James has him. I had to bring him. You probably heard him. Everybody probably heard him."

"That's okay," he said, "I want my mom to say hello to you."

Just then another thundercloud exploded overhead. I jerked my head the wrong way and saw that the cave was lit to display an open coffin with someone in it. I sang backward through my nose and teetered. The man I had never met was an old version of Caspar.

"Oh, Cas," I said, sobbing into his chest as he held me, "I'm so sorry." I wanted to explain the many things I was sorry for—including not being there for him sooner, bringing my brother, my Halloween witch hair—but I couldn't say words. Caspar held me until I managed to stop heaving, as if we were alone in that awful place.

I didn't say anything to his mom who was very busy with the receiving line. I turned and squeezed my way through the clusters of people. I don't know how many of them I bounced against or pushed past, but at one point I was face-to-face with Patrick Torno, who, without his baseball cap, looked older and more evil.

I tried to find Pan and the baby. I looked for the nearest way out rather than the way I had come in, so I was staring at a hearse as I bounded out a side door. The front passenger door opened, and I screamed as Pan got out with Paolo, as if they had returned from the dead.

The storm kept coming, juggling rain and lightning and thunder. I grabbed the umbrella from Pan and shouted, "Run for the store. It's closer than the car."

Inside the pharmacy, the two of us laughed almost maniacally. Then I was weeping, with Paolo's cries echoing mine.

"I'll never be invited to another death after this," I said.

"There'll be other opportunities," said Pan.

Tammie found her way to us. I had never been so glad to see her.

Chapter 24

I didn't call Caspar the rest of the week that he was absent from school. I just waited, unsure what he would think of me. Who would want to keep seeing a girl who dragged her screaming baby brother to his dad's calling hours, a girl in blue jeans who took a look at the body, burst into tears and ran out.

The next Saturday night was the second without him, and I seemed to have returned to my previous social life. If it weren't for Pan stopping by during the day to make sure I was still sane, the work hours would have seemed endless. But just before I left the store, Caspar called me. He sounded the same as he always did, even and steadily paced. He said it was nice of me to have come to the viewing. Before I could object and explain what a true mess I had been, he asked, "Can you come over?"

When I called home to tell Mom I was going straight to Caspar's, she said she would drive me in the truck. She brought a dish of baked ziti she had made to express her sympathy. I did not want this ziti, but I couldn't tell her no. When Caspar opened the cellar entrance and saw me posing with my casserole, he actually laughed, deep like early thunder. Shyly he waved to Mom, then guided me inside. He took the stupid dish and put it in the kitchenette's mini-refrigerator, then put his arms around me.

"I'm so sorry, Cas," I said. "For everything."

He was not in the mood for words. Neither was I. It had been too long since we'd held each other. That's what led to us not stopping where we usually stopped. I hesitated, thinking it was sacrilegious, like doing it in church. But it was his church, and he was the lead mourner. As usual, there were no sounds from upstairs.

I showed him the strips of condoms Pan had given to me.

"You won't think less of me for carrying them around all this time?" I asked.

He smiled. "We'd have to do it twenty times to need that many," he said.

"I don't have to be home till midnight," I said.

~

"I'm so happy to have you here," he said after. "It's been surreal."

"Uh, I'm sorry for what a nut I was at your dad's service."

"What do you mean? It was really kind of you to be there for me."

"It was raining and Paolo was even louder than usual, so I had to leave."

"That's okay. I didn't want to put you through any more of that than necessary."

"I made such a fool of myself, crying and all. Your mom must think I'm a flake."

"Nonsense. She didn't even see you."

"Okay."

"I kept thinking I wanted to keep you separate from all of that."

There was no point apologizing further. This was about his loss, not my lack of social elegance.

We lay together, silent for a long while.

"My brothers showed up," he finally said, turning on his side. "They came for a few minutes."

"That must have been awkward."

"They looked really uncomfortable, as if they didn't know how to behave or who to talk to. They stuck to themselves mostly. They made each other laugh."

"Really?"

"Not hilarious laugher, but nervous. They barely spoke to anyone else."

"I guess that means they're speaking to each other, anyway," I said.

"They said hello to me. More like 'hey' or something like that. I'm taller than both of them. They took off, and that's probably the last time I'll ever see them."

"Cas."

"I don't believe they said anything to my mom. I haven't asked her. There's too much going on for her right now."

"How's she doing?"

"She's amazing. She keeps busy all day and all night with what needs to be done."

"I guess that helps."

"She's always been that way. She knows how to take care of things. Even terrible things. Now you have to take care of me."

"I will."

"I thought about you a lot. I kept thinking, when this is all over, I will have Nia with me again."

I was ready to fill his locker with candy hearts and decorated brownies.

"How is James? I can't tell you how much it meant to me

that he was there."

"Yeah, he's a real friend," I said, thinking of him and Paolo in the hearse.

"I have to admit, I never really know how to approach him. Sometimes he seems to like me, and other times I feel like he's not listening."

"We talked through a bunch of things on the Cape, and he's cool. He's working on his jealousy."

"What is he jealous about?"

"You know, you and me," I said, wishing I had not said it.

"But he's not interested in you. That way."

"And don't I know it."

"What?"

"Nothing. He's not jealous because he wants to be my boyfriend. It's because we're best friends, he and I."

"Now you've got me confused."

"He was feeling left out because of the time you and I were spending together. Just a little. Now he's over it."

"You did go on vacation with him, after all."

"Yeah, and I told him I have room in my life for both of you."

"There's no reason you shouldn't."

"See why I like you? You understand everything."

"I would like to understand him better."

"I think he assumes all the boys in this town hate him."

"But he doesn't let anyone get to know him. A lot of people in school would like him if they had the opportunity, I'm sure."

"I agree. But I can't force him. I would like you to get to know each other. He's not so bad."

"I don't think he's bad at all," Caspar said with a slight annoyance. "I think he's very smart. Very articulate in class. That's mainly where I hear him talk, even though I'm sitting right there at lunch."

"He needs a little time," I said. "Just some time. Don't worry about it. He's going to his prom in Buckingham Heights, and I'm going to mine with you."

"But you said—"

"No argument," I said. "I want you to relax."

He lay on his back.

"I'll do exactly as you say," he said. "I don't want to listen to my own head for a while."

Chapter 25

When my junior year had started, the prom meant nothing to me. I didn't even think of it, anymore than I would have considered pole vaulting. Now I was kind of enjoying the complications leading up to it. I'd had two boys ask me. The second of the two wanted me to go as a real date, and the first now wanted me to go with the second to console him. Unpredictability could be enjoyable in an odd way.

This upcoming event had an unforeseen effect in that Mom, Pan, and I became a team for a short while as we shopped for a dress. There was a Day-Mart on the outskirts of town and there was also a Dress Shack. But Pan wouldn't have it.

"We are not shopping for anything in Mungers Mills," he said, "except bedbugs."

Mom jumped at the chance to go to one of the quality malls. This normally would have required a variety of babysitters: Usually when she wanted to go out and I couldn't stay with Paolo, she would lull him to sleep before the victim arrived, and when she returned, the babysitter would look like she hadn't slept in five days, take her money, and never return calls. But this time we had a repeat performer, who only made one comment about him being "a little fussy."

Mom was more of a kid than either of us. Pan bought her smoothies, gelato, bags of mixed candy. Shopping with the girls might seem like a stereotypical role for him. But he was all business, as if we were buying a car and had to be wary of sexist salesmen. Not just any guy could offer a masculine perspective while having the patience to shop for clothes with two women. He and Mom were determined to find the dress that would make me look magnificent.

But it began to look like there was no team on earth that could pull that off. The fun we had softened the repeated blows of seeing myself in a mirror wearing something I shouldn't. I did not have an evening gown body. Nothing flowed or draped on me. Material clung like gauze bandaging, emphasizing every unflattering lump and swerve. Plus-size shops were of no help either, since I wasn't a plus size. I was odd-sized, for which there were no special stores.

Pan and Mom were honest about each try, and tried to shift the blame.

"No one would look good in that. Bad cut," Mom said about one dress that made me look seventy.

"Court jester," Pan said about another, and then later, "Medieval serving wench. Who designs this stuff?"

Every dress was a mistake or a costume, including one where I looked like a ten-year-old bulging out of her mom's clothes.

When we decided that white would complement my rich skin tone, I tried on a gown that was so staticky, my hair was pointing at the ceiling by the time I was in it. Pan flinched when I came out of the dressing room. I forced him to tell me exactly why it was wrong.

"You know those ghost detector shows?" he started, and I cut him off. That supernatural sight led to a huddle where we settled on black, always a slenderizing and understated color for any occasion.

"Put it back on the rack," Mom said as she looked at me, "for the next Sicilian mourner."

This pursuit was doomed.

"We'll have one made," Mom said.

"Yeah," said Pan. "Why should we rely on the fashion gulags?"

"No, it's hopeless," I said.

"My friend Lynn knows someone in town who does custom wear," Mom said. "We'll get an estimate."

"Thanks, Mom, but I'm not paying to have a dress made for a stupid dance."

"Don't worry about it, honey," Mom said. "I'll pay. I want you to have a special night."

"Mama's right," Pan said.

"We barely have the cash to pay the babysitter when we get home," I said. "No, let's just go." Failure pressed on my trachea. "There's no point."

"We'll at least check her out, the dressmaker," Mom said. "That's final."

The retail gods must have heard her because we did find a dress that evening. It was at the fiftieth women's clothing store in the mall, which I would have ignored if Mom hadn't walked in. Pan found a dark blue dress with small, inconspicuous white designs. I had no faith when he insisted I try it on.

"It'll look better on you, Pan," I said. "Go ahead."

"Get in there this instant, young lady," he said, taking my arm and walking me and my latest adversary toward the dressing room.

Once I got it on, I was quite surprised to find myself wearing a dress instead of a fitted sheet. I tore out of the dressing room in case it was an illusion.

"That's it!" Mom said, and turned me around. "Oh, Nia, you can wear it more than once, too. It's formal, but not bridesmaid formal."

"I believe we have a winner," Pan said.

After sufficient ogling, Mom and Pan sent me back to the dressing room to take it off. I noticed the price tag dangling and grabbed it. Ninety-nine dollars. Not a lot for a dress in real life, but way beyond me. I sat down on the bench and kicked at some pins on the floor. I felt weak and tired and thought about curling up for a nap before reversing the good news.

Mom was on to me right away. "What's wrong?"

I tried sounding casual. "It's too expensive. Really, it's okay."

She grabbed the price tag. Her face fell, but then she forced a smile and said, "That, my dear, is a bargain."

"Mom, no, I can't afford it."

"We're buying it," she said. "I have a charge card. That's what they're for."

"Maaaa, I don't want you to."

"No argument," she said. "We've been looking long enough, and this is perfect on you. The story's told."

She was already on her way to the register. Pan and I followed. I did not want that dress. I thought of my dad at work, oily and exhausted, trying to appease customers. I could not wear it in good conscience.

The woman at the register scanned it. I couldn't look at the little screen.

"Forty-two thirty-seven," she said. Now I did look, and

those were the numbers.

"Oh," Mom said, trying not to sound thrilled.

"Sixty percent off," the cashier said. "It's a good deal."

"At that price she'll take two," said Pan. The woman looked up, vaguely interested, but I shook my head.

On the way home, we had that light spirit you get from a feel-good movie. For once, I'd gotten away with something, two things, really. Despite the conspiracy of the fashion industry, I had found a nice dress to wear. And even though it was made of something other than polyester, it had cost less than fifty bucks.

"Don't tell anyone we got it on sale," I warned Pan as he drove us home. "I want the girls to think I spent a thousand."

"You keep forgetting I have no one to tell, Nia."

"I can't believe it was so cheap," I said.

"Inexpensive," Mom said from the backseat. "Not cheap. It's quality."

"I would have bought you that dress myself for a hundred bucks," Pan said. "You looked amazing. That boy better appreciate you."

"He better not break up with me until it's been officially worn," I said.

"That's right," Mom said. "We didn't go to all this trouble for nothing."

I leaned over and kissed Pan's cheek. He kissed me back.

"You kids confuse me," Mom said.

"What do you mean, Mama F?" Pan asked.

"In my day the girl just married the guy and ignored he was gay."

"Really?" I asked. "What was the point?"

She sighed. "At least she got a good-looking husband for a while."

Chapter 26

Pan had a prom date, back in Buckingham Heights, with an old friend.

"Nothing romantic," he told me. "But he doesn't want to go alone."

Some of the girls at my school were approaching the prom with a ferocious intensity. I'd never had much interest in extracurricular activities, especially social ones. If things had been different, I would have worked at the pharmacy on prom night, possibly a little agitated about what the event—like Valentine's Day—represented.

Fortunately, Caspar picked me up in his dad's Lincoln Town Car instead of the red pickup. He took me to Flora's on the Lake which was outside of town and had a pretty view of the water. I ate with precision because I didn't want to spill anything on my only dress. I suppose it was just as well that the portions were the size of hors d'oeuvres.

I had been worried about Caspar seeing the inside of my house, and had spent too much of the day scrubbing the living room. You can't really scrub a room like that without it crumbling in places, but I tried to make it presentable. I took the whole place apart. I considered throwing away the cardboard Christmas fireplace we kept up all year, but it wasn't mine to toss. I powdered the carpet and sprayed the upholstery. When I got things reassembled, it was clear that what the living room really needed was all its contents thrown out, including the walls and floorboards. But that kind of overhaul was not going to happen by six-thirty.

The shifting of Caspar's emotions was always very hard to detect, but he was definitely nervous. He certainly didn't act like he was summing up how many bars down the economic graph my house was from his. He told me later that he had been uneasy about seeing my parents again. Mom was fine, though. She had gotten the new babysitter to take Paolo for the evening. And she wore nothing on her head. She brushed away tears as she clicked photo after photo, documenting that dress. Dad was his usual self, looking like he'd come to arrest somebody. At least he was all cleaned up. Working on the house, I'd obsessed about whether he would take a shower when he got home from work. He was sparkling when Caspar arrived, and I gave him and Mom unrestrained hugs before we left.

I should have felt like Cinderella arriving with her tall, athletic prince at the Courtesy Inn where the dance was held . But things got off to a bad start and only worked their way up to mediocre.

When Caspar and I walked into the lobby, Amanda was taking tickets at the door. She didn't have a date, which bothered me since she ought to have had one. I hadn't said much to her about going with Caspar, because it was so last-minute and because I didn't want her to feel bad. She wanted to be part of the event, so she sat there taking people's tickets and greeting them as if she were happy to.

Sitting next to her was sullen Amy Conrad who, not-sosurprisingly, wasn't coupled either. Amy's usual facial expression was sour. But when she saw Caspar do this old-fashioned thing of putting out his arm for me to take, her tiny body shuddered with laughter and she turned her head, as if we wouldn't be able to see her. My heart pumped lightning, and I wanted to turn and go home. Instead, I put my arm through Caspar's, and we headed into the banquet room. I don't know if Caspar saw her laughing, but I wasn't mentioning it.

From that point on, the only connection I had with Cinderella was the feeling of being exposed. We were on display because everyone was. People alternately showed off and analyzed each other's showing off. There was no banquet in the banquet room, just an apricot punch. I didn't think apricots and punch had any connection before this, and now I knew why. One sip of the syrupy drink was enough to make me misplace my cup.

Caspar and I danced to a few slow songs, and I danced with a couple of my old Holy Redeemer girlfriends to faster numbers, and the whole time I kept wondering when the magic would begin. When he wasn't dancing with me, Caspar sat like an immense wallflower. I thought of asking him to ask Amanda for a dance, but somehow I knew they would be awkward together, especially since she was even shorter than me. There was a prolonged court ceremony to endure.

I don't know why I expected the prom to be more than it was, but ultimately I did not love or hate it. I should have been grateful that instead of being alone at work, I was actually part of the festivities. Instead, I was bored. I wished Pan would crash the party with his date. We could have had some defiant fun—me dancing with him, him dancing with another guy—although I don't know how Caspar would have gone for it.

Finally, I accepted that the fireworks were not going to happen and went over to him and asked if he was ready to go. He smiled for the first time since we'd arrived.

We skipped the after-parties Caspar had been invited to. Since we were both starving, we stopped and shared a footlong sub on the way back to his place. I wore two paper napkins on my chest to protect my dress. Later, after some very pleasant gymnastics in his basement, he drove me home. His car idled in front of my house while we sat talking.

"Did you have a nice evening?" he asked, looking mournful.

"With you I did," I said. "I could have lived without seeing Isabella Cooper burst into tears when she was crowned queen."

"I agree," he said. "It was very boring. Not you, of course."

"That's good."

"No, I mean that prom court. It took so long. All that forced anticipation."

"Yeah," I said, "and then Patrick Torno was called as a knight of the court."

"At least he wasn't king. Not that it matters." He kissed me. "I love you."

I was slightly startled by this, but knew enough not to reply with, "You do?" Instead I asked, "Why do you look so sad, Cas? I'm afraid to leave you like this."

"I was thinking about my dad. It comes up at the strangest times."

"Then I guess I'll have to stay right here with you."

"No, I'm okay. You made the night worthwhile."

"You did, too. For me."

"You're my queen."

"Don't say that in front of James, please."

Caspar looked dumbfounded.

"Just a joke," I said. "Are you sure you're okay? Do you want to come in again? It's no problem. I just have to warn you about fifteen different things if you do."

"No, I'd better get home."

I got out. My dress was a little rumpled now. "Drive safe in this thing," I said, tapping the car's roof.

"Oh, don't worry," he said. "My dad used to say it has enough air bags to levitate."

One relief was that my parents were both asleep instead of waiting with their fingers poised on the light switch.

Despite the blah dance, I felt strangely contented, like things had been accomplished. I had done the prom bit and could dismiss it once and for all. Hopefully, Pan's evening had been better, and I was happy that he hadn't sat home alone. I loved my dress. It was too good for this occasion, but there would be others. I looked forward to my normal life of jeans and the pickup. Not adventurous, but comforting, and for the time being, parallel.

Pan called me Sunday morning, way early. Instead of us gushing over our big evenings out, he explained his own lackluster experience, showing up at the Buckingham Heights prom with his friend, both in tuxes. If he had hoped for some controversy, he hadn't gotten it dancing with another boy there.

"A transgender guy was elected to the court," he said. "And there was no king and queen stuff."

"Can you imagine that happening here?" I asked.

"Not much happens here," he said.

"Nope," I said. "Tonight definitely proves that."

Chapter 27

There was less than a month left of school. One day while we were eating, Caspar asked what I wanted to do Saturday night. This was a lapse in etiquette because he and I and Pan never discussed our plans in front of the person who was not included.

"I don't know," I said. "Watch a movie?"

"Is there anything new at the theater? We could drive somewhere."

"Not sure. I'll have to look."

"Let's go to my house. I have movies."

I really didn't want him pursuing this. But then he said, "I mean the three of us. James, my dad's collection is huge. Blu-ray. Ultra HD Blu-ray. Old-fashioned DVDs. VHS if it comes to that. Plus every streaming service out there. There's got to be something we can all agree on."

Neither of us answered.

Caspar looked very concerned. "Do you have something else to do?"

I took a bite of my sandwich, but I tasted nothing.

"I wish I did have something to do," Pan said. He paused,

looked at me, then back at Caspar. "Not because I don't want to come to your house. That's not what I meant."

"No, I didn't think that. Let's do it, then," Caspar said.

Caspar bent to take a spoonful of his soup. I didn't look at Pan, but I felt a little expansion inside, as if something like elation was stretching.

~

Pan came to my house, where Caspar was going to pick us up. We were sitting in my living room, Mom's delighted attention on Pan who was swinging Paolo. Dad came home from work looking tired and grim. His mood was not improved by seeing Pan tossing his son around and Paolo loving it. He didn't say anything, but Pan stopped, and Paolo let us all know it. Paolo didn't run to Dad to greet him; he insisted that Pan continue the acrobatics. But Pan tried to move away. It didn't work. Paolo clung to him.

"That's enough, Pow," said Dad, but Paolo didn't care.

"Dad," I said, as Paolo howled at Pan. But this only made Dad more frustrated and he yelled, "Pow!"

We heard a car horn. Pan and I were leaving no matter who was honking it.

Mom pulled Paolo off Pan so we could get away. "Great, Tony," she said. "Just when I had a few minutes of quiet. Go take a shower."

Pan was fidgety in the truck, not composed and distant the way he usually was around Caspar. He sat next to the door, the three of us squashed in together.

When we got to Caspar's, Pan and I sat in the basement while Caspar went upstairs. Pan was unusually quiet.

"This is a huge place," he said with a slight quaver in his voice.

Caspar brought down sandwiches, chips, soda, and brownies his mom had set aside for us. At first there was no conversation while we ate. I thought about suggesting we start the movie, then decided not to meddle. Pan finally said to me, "It's good. Not like Mama Fazzino's cooking, but not untasty."

"Is her mom a good cook?" Caspar asked.

"She's excellent. Gourmet. She can make something delicious with any ingredients she has handy. I'm tempted to bring her lawn clippings some day to test my theory."

Caspar had his mouth full, so he added a muffled, "My mom cooks by cell phone."

For some reason this struck Pan as hilarious. His laughter made food burst out of his mouth, which made Caspar laugh.

After coughing out the scraps he had choked on, Pan said, "Do you still want me to stay? I mean, after I almost yakked all over the place?"

"There was no vomit that I could see," Caspar said like a reassuring doctor.

Pan relaxed a little after that, but he wasn't entirely unwound. We selected a movie. It helped that we chose a terrible one.

Caspar tried to adjust the settings on the TV because depending on the scene, the actors were either silhouettes or blanched. Once when a man lit a cigarette, the entire screen went white. In general, smoking seemed to fog up the camera lens. Finally, Caspar figured it was a problem with the filming, not his equipment.

"My dad liked independent films. Sometimes they are real low budget. Maybe too low. Should we try something else?"

"We can make fun of it," Pan said.

So we watched, and laughed where we weren't supposed to. The movie was so bad that it wasn't long before Pan and Caspar were narrating it.

I didn't try to narrate, because they had a rhythm. Still, it might have been the best fun I'd had in forever. I felt a little high, completely stoned on sugar and foolishness.

Caspar offered to drive us home after we had laughed ourselves to coughing fits and eaten way too much. I knew he probably wanted some alone time with me, but I didn't think the evening could get any more perfect. So Pan and I did what we always did and walked, repeating the dumbest lines from the movie all the way.

Chapter 28

I wanted to be left alone at work the next day, to enjoy my recent memories. But it was a particularly busy day for Polaski's Pharmacy. Midafternoon, when there was finally a lull and I was thinking about calling Caspar just to say hi, I had quite a surprise. Patrick Torno walked in with two elderly people who must have been his grandparents. Or great-grandparents. Maybe greater. The three of them didn't really walk in. It was a production for him getting them in the door with all their yipping and banging. The grandfather walked with a cane that had four feet. Torno appeared not to see me as he and his huddle made their way.

I felt like a detective, observing him without being observed. I wondered who had exchanged souls with him that he was so patient helping these old people around the store. He sounded like an old man himself, repeating each item several times and how much it cost, explaining what it was for. Once in a while he would scold one of them for talking too loud, or both of them for arguing, or for a near-miss with a shelf of colognes.

Pan's timing was either terrible or razor-sharp because he

came in while the trio was negotiating a second aisle.

"Guess what? I have another date with my father," he said. "I'm going to beg you to come with me."

I put my index finger to my lips.

"Is Tammie—"

I grabbed him so I could get close to his ear. "Patrick Torno is here. With his grandparents, I think. They're both a hundred."

The devil smiled out of his face.

There was a small outburst, then the three of them bumbled their way to the front again. Torno must have wished he could fly when he saw Pan. The old woman called to me, "We need a urinal. My husband can't get out of bed fifteen times a night."

"Aisle four," I said. "Three-quarters of the way down on the left. With the home health equipment."

Pan turned and fixed a look at Torno. "Aisle four, sir," he said.

Torno, very harsh now, said to the old ones, "Stay here. I'll get it," and jogged off.

He came back with the urinal box, holding it at his side to camouflage it. The old man took the box, examined it, then dropped it. Pan picked it up and handed it back.

"You just hold on to the handle here?" the man asked, pointing to the picture on the box.

"You put it next to the bed and use it during the night," the woman answered.

She took the box and opened the top, fumbling a little. Finding the urinal inside encased by thin plastic, she tried to grab the handle. She dropped it, and then the box too, and Pan again bent to pick them up. Torno looked at the floor. Pan unwrapped the urinal and held it out by the handle to the man. The wife took it again and said, "See? Like this. You hold this part and you pee into the tube part."

"Then what do you do with it?" asked the man.

"Well, you don't hand it to me," she said. They both laughed. "You put it down and go back to sleep."

"But it'll spill all over. How do you keep it from spilling? That's just what we need."

"No, look," said Pan as if he'd done this before. "There's a cap, and you close it when you're finished. Peeing."

"Oh, I see," said the man, and took the urinal from his wife. "So you snap the lid back on like a can of dog food."

"Just like it," said Pan. "But don't put it in the refrigerator." The old people laughed again. Not their grandson.

"Let's go. They've got other things to do," said the man.

"We should get two," the woman said. "He loses everything."

"Oh, you," said the old man.

Pan took the urinal from him and put it back in the box, then brought it over to the counter. The man turned to Torno and said, "Would you like one, too, Paddy? We said we'd treat you to something."

The woman sounded like a wolf baying when she laughed. "Oh, for heaven's sake," she said. "You stop teasing."

"I'm just saying. He'll be an old man, too, someday."

Gravity was having a marked effect on Torno's face. Any second now it would sag to his toes. I wished we could access the store's surveillance camera so Pan and I could play the scene over and over. It was wicked, but I rationalized that if we never told anyone, we should at least be able to savor this memory. Pan wasn't going to report him and Samsonite in school, so secret retribution would have to do.

"Will that be it?" I asked, reaching to scan the box.

Torno's voice came through a pool of phlegm. "We have to

get the prescriptions."

"Oh, okay," I said.

"What?" asked the woman.

Torno didn't clear his throat. He sounded like he was waking up from anesthesia. "The medicine. We have to go to the back and get the medicine."

"That's what we came here for," said the man. "The pee bottle was your idea, Rose."

"And I'm glad I remembered," she said.

"You can pay for these," I said, "along with your prescriptions, in the back."

Pan took the box and said softly, "Need some help?"

Torno grabbed it from him.

"Have a good day," Pan said.

"Every day on this side of the grass is a good day," the man said.

"Shut up and let's go," said the woman.

Then the grandparents forgot about us and were bumping their noisy way toward the back of the store. Torno followed them out of view.

Pan looked like he had just seen paradise.

"What an afternoon it's been," he said.

"Go home," I said. "I'll call you tonight."

"But there's no back exit. That they know of. They have to go by us again."

"That's exactly why you have to leave. He's had enough for one day."

"What?"

"Go on. Git."

"I can't believe you're ruining this for me."

"It's been a lot of fun, I agree. But enough is enough. Go."

"You're really kicking me out? I haven't even told you about the thing with my father."

There was another disturbance from the couple in the back of the store, then muffled arguing.

"I want to hear it," I said. "Every detail. I'll call you."

He snorted as he left. Then, outside, he pressed his nose against the window and batted his eyes. I turned away.

When Torno and his entourage made their way to the front again, he didn't look at me, and I said nothing to him. I had felt sorry for him about the urinal, and he'd been amazingly patient with his grandparents. I may have done the right thing by not letting Pan stay and gloat, but Patrick Torno wasn't getting anything else from me.

Chapter 29

I'd told Pan to pick me up the next morning at the corner of my street. Mom had not been as difficult about giving up her Saturday morning bowling as I'd expected.

"I suppose I could try taking Paolo with me to the lanes," she said. "He might throw the others off their game." I could see she was not going to try it.

"Pan promises to babysit next Saturday morning," I said. This was true, although Dad would not approve.

"It seems like a year away," she said. "Go. Be supportive. Tell him I'm thinking about him."

I went out when I heard a horn. Kevin was driving. He rolled down his window and said, "I'm just coming along for the ride." I got in and we were off.

~

When we got to the diner parking lot, we knew who Robertson was right away. His hair was a little darker, but he was definitely Pan's dad, standing by the railing of the diner entrance smoking a cigarette.

Before Kevin parked the car, Pan turned around to me.

"You're coming in."

"No."

"I mean it. I can't do this alone."

When the car stopped, we all got out, and Pan held on to me as we walked toward Robertson. There were awkward introductions.

"I'll be back in an hour," Kevin said.

Pan only let me go long enough to lunge at Kevin and give him a tight hug. Kevin whispered something, then gave him a be-strong look. I turned to follow Kevin back to the car. But Pan pulled me into the diner.

Robertson didn't seem to mind that I was crashing this lunch. When we sat down, Robertson took out another cigarette and lit it.

"I have one of these until I get caught," he said. "So, what do you kids think of this Congress we have?"

Thinking I was supposed to answer, I said, "Um, I—"

"You know what Will Rogers said about Congress? It opens with a prayer and closes with an investigation."

A waitress came over to our table. "You sneaky snake. You put that out or I'll slap your naughty hand."

"I'll light up the whole pack at that rate," Robertson said, winking at her and stubbing out his cancer stick. "What are we having, kids?"

I ordered a salad that came in a dish the size of a sleigh. Pan ordered a sandwich. Robertson had a giant burger platter. Although he did all the talking, which gave us plenty of time to eat, Pan and I both only picked at our food.

Robertson could have been talking to anyone with his monologue transitioning from one current event to another: "That's the way this country is run now. You've got two kinds of people running the government. Bad, and worse than bad."

He would be quiet just long enough to insert a mouthful of

food, then be back to it. He asked questions, then answered them himself. I nodded and smiled till it became automatic.

Finally he got off the political stuff. "James, your mother. I hope she's well. She was quite a firebrand when she was a girl. Very smart, beautiful. Accomplished. Your stepdad is a lucky guy, as are you."

That was an odd sentiment, considering this was the first time he'd seen his son since he was a toddler.

Despite all his talking, Robertson's plate was glimmering clean when he was done. I hadn't thought it was possible, but then he found a way to be even more obnoxious. When the check came, he examined it carefully and told us what we owed. I hadn't expected him to pay for my lunch, but this was his son.

Pan put down forty dollars. "For both of us," he said, his voice lifeless.

"Hold—wait—wait there. That's too much," Robertson said, looking at the check again.

"Keep it."

"Maybe you're right," Robertson said. "A little extra tip. She was a good girl, eh?"

When we got up to leave, he shook our hands like we had concluded a merger.

"James, I'm pleased to see you've turned into a fine young man. Your mother has done an excellent job with you, as I knew she would. Your stepdad too. And your girl is a peach."

Peaches were round and covered with fuzz. I hated him.

He did not suggest that he and Pan meet again or stay in touch. The business lunch was over, and more cigarettes were calling to him. Pan didn't have much chance to ask him any questions, didn't tell him I was not his girl or why.

Kevin was waiting, always reliable, and his reward was Pan being in the worst mood ever. He alternated between sullen silence and snapping at one or the other of us—for something we said, for the radio being too loud, for the car hitting potholes.

"Well, at least tell me what happened," Kevin said, "that you're so angry."

"Nothing happened," Pan said. "Literally nothing."

"For heaven's sake, Nia, what in the world did that man say?"

"He didn't really say anything. Just talked about the government, things like that the whole time."

"And he made us pay," Pan said. "Don't you think that if you were meeting your son for the first time in fourteen years, you would pay for his lunch? And maybe even his friend's, who came all this way with him?"

"I suppose I would."

"Jesus, Kevin, can you step on it? We're never going to get home. Nia has plans tonight."

I was practically choking on agitation by the time we got near our exit. After he'd slapped me down for the fifth time and Kevin for the millionth, I said, "You only have to look like him, James. You don't have to be the asshole he is."

That wasn't my style. Kevin caught my eye in the rearview mirror.

Pan's silence was almost shouting at us after that. But when we got back in the car after a rest area stop, he opened the back door and got in next to me. He put his head on my shoulder, resting it there until we got home.

Chapter 30

Pan was as subdued as I'd ever known him to be when we talked Sunday, and his mood had not changed by the next day at school. Samsonite didn't help matters any during Science and Society.

"Why don't they just face reality?" he asked. "Who wants to crap all the time? And who wants to kiss a girl who's puking up her lunch every day?"

We were in The Circle, this time discussing eating disorders. The subtopic of purgatives had gotten him excited. There was no groaning when he spoke. It was June after all, and he had us trained to wait it out.

But Caspar took everybody seriously. He shifted himself in his small seat, wrinkled his brow, and said, "I think the reality is they can't control it."

"Sure they can," said Samsonite. "No one's making them puke."

"I saw a documentary on the Nutrition Channel about it," Caspar continued. "They think there's some kind of abnormality in the way certain chemicals affect the brain."

"It's abnormal all right," said Patrick Torno, foreboding as a thunder cloud.

"There's no way I would go out with a girl like that," Samsonite said.

"No one's asking you to," said Caspar, and again he made people laugh without intending to. His grave expression didn't change, as if an idea was unfolding in his head. "Maybe there are things about our minds that we can't control. So, you can't expect people to make good decisions in those circumstances."

"Whatever," said Torno.

"Speaking of shitting all the time," Pan said, "have you considered a bedpan to complete the set?"

No one laughed at that cryptic outburst. The room suddenly felt soundproof.

Torno looked like Hell's race car was speeding out of his eyes.

"James?" Mrs. Mercado asked, puzzled.

"Come on, Paddy," Pan continued. "How are things in the land of incontinence?"

"James," Mrs. Mercado repeated, a bit stern now. She cleared her throat and sat up a little straighter. "Let's keep it relevant."

"You're worried about relevance?" Pan said to her. "With these two? The delusional duo?"

She stared at Pan with a mix of anger and hurt on her face.

"Everyone," she said, slightly unsteady, "is entitled to their opinion."

"And my opinion," Pan said, "is that some people aren't."

"Please," I whispered to him.

He took in a deep breath, appearing to collect himself. "I'm sorry," he said to her. "Carry on."

Normally, she would toss out a kid for such temerity, but Pan was a straight-A student, top of the class. It must have stung to have him question her judgment.

"We'll have to agree to disagree," she said, not quite finding her voice.

Pan looked up at the ceiling, then stretched his neck back and forth.

The rest of the period crept by like a dysfunctional family holiday. Barely anyone spoke. People avoided glances. The only thing I imagined I could hear was Torno's percolating blood. He stared at Pan as if programmed to kill.

The bell rang, like it was granting clemency.

"Have a blessed rest of your day," Pan said to Torno as we were leaving the room.

I was ready to put myself between them, call to Caspar if I had to. But Torno didn't say or do anything, which scared me more.

Chapter 31

Why didn't I make the connection that evening when I saw Samsonite and Torno pass by the store windows just a minute or so after Pan had left? Instead, I only thought it was unusual, and had a fleeting hope that they wouldn't run into each other. I went back to work organizing the paperback book and magazine section. People stood around reading them, but they seldom bought one.

Not long after Pan came back in, a bit wobbly. He looked scuffed up, smudges on his face and arms, his hair a wild mess. Worst was a trickle of blood from his nose drying a dirty brown.

"Pan, what?" Panic was growing inside me.

"I need something to clean up with." His voice was as self-possessed as always.

"What happened?" As I got close to him, ammonia blasted at me. "What is it?"

"Nothing."

Now I could see bruises too. Then I made the connection.

"Tell me, right now," I said, though I could guess the basics. I could have pulled my own hair for being so dim.

"I just need some paper towels or something."

"Tell me," I said with a ferocity I didn't know was in me. "What the hell is going on?"

"If you loves me," he said, "you won't ask any more questions."

He was not going to talk. I felt like I'd been tasered as I ran through the store. I managed to find a package of body wipes, big disposable ones for people who couldn't take a bath. I sped back to him. He waited as if nothing was out of the ordinary.

I opened the package and yanked out a few wet cloths. I started with his hair and face. He grabbed one and did his arms, casually. The fumes defied us. Really, he smelled like an alley wall. It was on his clothes, in his hair, and, as it turned out, in his mouth.

"I'm calling the police," I said, going for my phone. Nothing was going to stop me this time. But Pan grabbed it like he was closing his grip on a mosquito. I tried to grab it back.

"If you won't let me do it here, I'll call from home," I said. "Someone has got to stop those little freaks."

He held the phone high over me, which wasn't hard considering our heights. Then he handed it back, as if he trusted his own resolve more than mine.

"I just need to get changed and go home. Can we go to your house first? Clean up a little? No point in setting my mother off."

"I can't take this anymore. I can't watch you pretend nothing's happening. I can't." I gasped a few giant breaths. "It's too much."

He put his hand on my shoulder. "Please don't, baby. I'm okay, I really am. I just need a friend right now."

"No!" I turned away from him and pressed myself against

the counter.

Detective Tammie entered the scene.

"James, what's the matter with her? What happened to you? What's that smell?"

But I had no allegiance except to him. I stood straight, breathed in deep.

"Tammie, I have to go. He's been attacked and I'm taking him to the police station."

"But that'll leave us short-staffed."

"You know how to manage a register," I said, which stopped her next objection.

"Come on," I said, taking Pan's tacky arm. "We're going."

If Tammie protested, I didn't hear her and didn't care.

The police station was only a few blocks from the pharmacy. I almost hoped Samsonite and Patrick Torno were lurking. I would protect us. I had an older brother. I knew how to fight, and I wouldn't hesitate punching below the belt.

Pan had slowed down. Already I knew a different fight had begun.

"Nia, I can't go in there."

"They'll have to make a report. They'll find them."

"No, they won't," he said.

"Do you really think Samsonite can keep his mouth shut, of all people? As soon as they question him he'll squall like a baby."

"He's probably related to half the force," Pan said.

"No, this time we're doing the right thing, not the convenient thing."

He stopped. "Take me to your house and let me get cleaned up first."

"They'll need evidence. If you get cleaned up—"

"Please."

"We have to."

"Not like this," he said, his voice faltering for a second.

We began walking again, away from the station. After a couple of blocks, I said, "Will you at least tell me the story?"

"I don't want to relive it. Let's just say they didn't walk away nice and clean, either."

I could almost not stand this scrap-of-pride.

"They really should have planned it better," he said. When I didn't answer, he continued, "You're the best friend a person could ask for. What do you think of my new cologne?"

But nothing was funny. When we got to my house, I insisted he come in for a shower. He wouldn't budge farther than the porch.

"Don't let them know I'm here," he whispered. "Your father especially."

"Screw that," I said. I was not babysitting for Dad's limitations.

"No, he'll be disgusted with me."

"Why am I arguing with you, Pan? A crime has been committed and we're worrying about my dad?"

But I couldn't out him to my parents. He convinced me to throw his putrid clothes in the washer for a quick rinse so he could carry them home without the odor. I grabbed a long coat off the rack next to the side door and gave it to him. Then I took the hideous bundle into the cellar, hating Samsonite and Torno. If Torno ever walked into Polaski's again, even with the elderly in tow, I would call the cops and claim all three of them were shoplifting.

I tried to find something for Pan to wear. No one in my house was thin and tall, so there wasn't a lot to choose from. In the dryer I found a pair of Mom's sweat pants and one of Dad's undershirts. Both hung on Pan like he was a clothesline, and the legs of the pants rode up almost to his knees. I also brought wet washcloths and a big towel for him to use on his face, hair, and arms.

I told him again we were going to the police, but I knew it wasn't going to happen. If I had been thinking more clearly, I would have gotten Mom to back me up. Instead, we stayed on the porch while we waited for the washer.

Sitting tranquilly on the dilapidated steps in his absurd outfit, Pan was already looking down on the incident. I had lost again.

"You're doing the wrong thing," I said.

"We can't say anything about this. Not to Caspar even."

I wanted to tell Caspar in the worst way, what little I knew, but it was a violent impulse. I wanted him to grab Samsonite and Torno by their necks and pound their heads together like a pair of cartoon cymbals.

"Why?" I asked.

"I'll make sure they're taken care of," Pan said. "I'm not completely helpless, you know."

"You have a gun? Please don't have a gun."

"Guns are for amateurs."

"This is the last time I listen to you, I swear. I'm afraid for you. Terrified for you."

He leaned against me. He smelled okay now, his hair all wet tangles from the washcloths. "Only the good die young," he said. "I've got forever."

Chapter 32

To anyone else it would look like a perfect morning, the sun burning off the cool of the previous night. Everything was illuminated—the houses, the trees, anything against the sky. Normally I would think it was all beautiful, but I hated going to school knowing I would have to see Samsonite and Patrick Torno. And keep my mouth shut.

My life, for a few weeks, had been the way I wanted it—a best friend to walk me home and a boyfriend to kiss me good-bye. Companionship, real romance—as perfect as a girl from Mungers Mills could expect. But today the light was relentless. I felt like those two scumbags were hanging over my head, like a bill due for my short period of parallelism.

Evidently I was bearing the trepidation for both me and Pan, since he was in a light mood. I knew if I even mentioned the night before, he would ignore it.

"Are you playing today?" I asked when I saw the end of his tennis racket sticking out of his bag.

"I'm taking a lesson after school."

"I wish I had learned how to play. If the courts here had been kept up, you could have coached me."

"I believe in your potential," he said.

Pan wasn't being cautious or wary, looking around to see where Samsonite and Torno might be perched. Knowing Caspar would be in school chipped away a little of my fear, but still I wanted to skip out before the day was through. I'd never done that, but I couldn't stand the thought of seeing them. I realized with despair that now Pan couldn't report them until they did something else, and the school year was ending. In Science and Society, Torno turned his evil head our way a couple times, but not Samsonite, who for once said nothing.

After the final bell, Pan reminded me of his tennis lesson and told me I should go on home, that he was staying to work with our gym teacher.

"Oh," I said. "I thought you were taking a lesson after school, somewhere else. Are you telling the truth, or is there another girl in your life now?"

"Believe it or not, I'm going to practice my swing with Mr. Hicks," he said.

"What?"

"Yeah, spring was so wet that I've missed a lot of practice time. I need to get back into condition. I don't want to lose everything because I moved here."

"Mr. Hicks? What does he know about tennis?"

"He's a PE teacher, or as close to one as you get in Mungers Mills. He used to give lessons. Anyway, gotta go."

I was afraid to leave him alone. "Can I come with you? Just for a few minutes?"

"And watch?" he asked. "You'll be bored. Go home."

I followed him out the side loading area where kids waited for the buses.

"Where are you going?" I asked. "The gym office is down the next hall."

"I'll call you tonight," he said, "several times."

I thought I understood: Pan was disguising his fear. He didn't have a lesson at all, and going out a more obscure exit might keep him from getting attacked again. But being where no one could see Torno and Samsonite jump him was a risk, too. I wanted to assure him it was okay to be afraid, but I knew better than to bring the subject up.

There was a picnic table where two wings of the building made a corner, probably a hideout for the bus drivers between runs. Pan walked over and sat on the top.

"What are we doing here?" I asked.

"I'm going to wait here for him. He said he'd be free at four."

"Mr. Hicks?"

"Yeah. Go ahead home. I intend to bother you all night at chez pharmacie."

I felt a twinge of discomfort at the back of my neck.

"Pan, I'm confused. Are you meeting a guy here? I can handle it. As long as he's not thirty, or something awful like that."

"No. Go on. Go. I am one hundred percent groovy."

"Okay. Call me."

I turned toward the door near the loading area.

"Hey, Boz-o-leum and Paddy," I heard Pan call as if he were a coach, "get your faggoty asses over here." Only then did I realize what he'd been planning, and turned back. I had to get him out of there.

Samsonite looked, then looked away. But like an animal lured by food, Torno charged toward Pan. Samsonite followed, slower.

Pan understood the element of surprise, too, because before they got close to us, he turned his back on them. Then he was facing them, bringing the tennis racket down on

Torno's head. With coordinated precision he did the same to Samsonite. As they shouted their disbelief, I tried to grab the racket from behind, but Pan connected with their bodies as if I were not there. They couldn't get their balance to rush him as he laid on more blows. Samsonite drew back, covering his face. Standing like a crumpled sapling, Torno looked up at Pan, dazed. But Pan was not retreating. He brought the netting down again and again—on heads, on butts, on backs, on arms. Sounding like he was calling to himself, Torno cried, "My face. My face."

A bus driver charged toward us. I shouted for Pan to stop as he continued swinging, now at the air around him. I forced myself toward him, ducking and dodging, and grabbed the racket. The bus driver was blowing a tirade out of his mouth.

I held the racket as high as I could. "Go away!" I said. He drew back, but I was the terrified one. I didn't know this girl using my body.

"Give me that!" he shouted.

"Get back," I said. "They're the ones who started this." I pointed to Samsonite and Torno, now both on the ground. Torno was crawling as if searching for a contact lens.

"You give me that thing," the bus driver yelled, "or I'll shove it so far through your ear it'll come out the other side." He spat every word. He lunged for me, but I stepped back. "Gimme that thing or I'm gonna drive this bus right over you two, do you understand me?"

"It's just a tennis racket," I said, hoarse and desperate. "Leave us alone. Please, just leave us alone."

He was out of words now, so he actually made a sound like a howl. A crowd was starting to gather.

The last thing I saw before the bus driver fell was his giant red face coming toward me. Then he was on his knees and falling sideways. It appeared that between the two of us, Pan and I had killed three people in less than forty-five seconds.

I took Pan by the arm and pulled him away. I was stronger than I knew, because he was like pulling a broom. As we were running I could hear, but not see, Mrs. Guten on the scene yelling, "We have an emergency situation here. I need you to get on your buses, now. Move it out. On your buses. They need to be out of the way. Move!"

I must have made quite the picture, the short warrior goddess with her spear in one hand and a boy in the other. Once we were far enough from the school, hidden in a patch of woods near an abandoned gas station, Pan pulled away from my grip. I sat on the ground, sucking air. He stood, breathing deep but not spent.

"You okay?" he asked.

"Better than ever," I managed to gasp out.

"Guten's got some pipes on her, doesn't she?"

I tried to catch my breath.

"You didn't have to do that," he said. "I could have taken care of myself."

"That's what I was afraid of."

"I told you to go home, Nia."

"Why did you do that? Why did you hit them? You're going to spend senior year in a detention home."

"It has possibilities."

"Shut up. Do you know what they would do with a kid who looks like you? I'm not kidding."

"I'm sorry."

I looked up at him. The sun throbbed without mercy through the trees. He sat down beside me, put his hand on my forehead.

"I'm not kidding either, Nia. I am so, so sorry."

Chapter 33

I expected the cops to pick us up on our way to Pan's. When they didn't, I waited for them to come to his house. I almost called in to work thinking I would be in jail before I got anywhere near the pharmacy. Pan was not concerned as he drove me home.

"You didn't do anything wrong," he said. "Stop worrying. You won't be spending your summer in Cell Block H."

"You've got to tell them about Samsonite and Torno," I said. "You don't have a choice now."

"Listen, if anything happens and in any way, shape, or form you are implicated in this, I will make my case against them. I'll spill every detail. I promise. But only if."

"No, don't ask me to keep my mouth shut anymore."

"If not, if it's just me in trouble, which it will be, then please, don't say a word. I don't want to be the cause célèbre of Mungers Mills. I don't want the one newspaper reporter in town writing about the school's pitiful gay boy."

No matter how many times we had this argument, he was still wrong, completely. But too much had happened and I had no energy.

There were no cops. There were, however, many phone calls, and the next morning Dad, Mom, and I were in Dr. Jackson's office. Mom's face was as stony as Dad's usually was. I couldn't look at either of them.

When Dr. Jackson motioned for them to sit in a pair of chairs in front of his desk, Mom defiantly pulled up a third.

"Nia, sit here," she said, and I obeyed. I sat between her and Dad, and hung my head. I wanted to arrange my hair over my face, look out through the strands.

Dr. Jackson spoke in a low and dry tone about school policy, with Mrs. Guten nodding her head. Mom and Dad said nothing.

"Nia," Mrs. Guten said in the most soothing voice she could manage, "we're concerned about you. We want you to take care of yourself, be careful who you hang around with. This was a very dangerous situation, a student who gets violent like that." She looked at Mom and Dad and added, "Things are not the same as when we went to school."

"That boy has never given us one moment's trouble," Mom said.

"JoAnne," Dad said, putting a hand on her arm.

"He may need anger management—" Mrs. Guten started.

Mom yanked her arm away from Dad. "My daughter," she said, soft but steady, "does not need advice."

"It's for her own protection," Dr. Jackson said. "James told us there was no provocation."

"We all know the real story here," Mom said. "I can't afford lawyers, but that doesn't mean I don't understand things."

"Is Nia in trouble?" Dad asked. "Yes or no? Suspension?"

"No," said Dr. Jackson, "but she didn't give the racket to Mr. Snibley when he asked for it."

"Mr. Snibley was threatening her," Mom said. "He made

threats to her, which I will repeat to the police myself if I have to."

"Is she suspended?" Dad asked. "My wife and I would like to know."

"No," said Mrs. Guten. "We just want to know if she has anything to say about why James might have behaved the way he did toward these two boys. James's parents claim there must have been bullying. But he won't tell us. If we don't have a complaint, we have nothing to investigate."

Dad looked at me. His eyes were searching, sad. "Nia, do you have something to say?"

"Honey?" Mom said, touching my hand.

I didn't feel anything at that moment, not guilt or fear or remorse, not a thing. So I didn't understand why I was trembling.

"No."

"Then we are finished here," Mom said, and we got up to leave. Dad followed and shut the door behind us. Mom put her arm around me as we walked to the parking lot.

"Snibley," she murmured.

"Nia, that boy could have gotten you in a lot of trouble," Dad said.

"Drop it, Tony," Mom said. "I swear to God."

~

That night I found out from Pan that his experience in the office had made mine look like a birthday party. Ada, Pan's mom, had smiled all the way through it, but a deranged smile. Kevin had told them that the school had not protected their son, and Pan was being punished for standing up for himself.

"We have a zero tolerance policy here, Mr. Ashford," Dr. Jackson had said. "James has proven to be a danger to other students."

"You don't think James has been in danger? You know the score."

Mrs. Guten had said that they wanted to investigate any claims, and that Torno and Samsonite would be punished if they were proven. But Pan had never complained about them, not all year, and he was still saying nothing.

"So, it's James's fault," Kevin had said. "If he had just told on his classmates, this never would have happened. Of course he doesn't want to say anything. You know how these things work. Don't be naive. How can you expect a teenage boy to do your jobs for you?"

Dr. Jackson had replied that considering the circumstances, Pan was lucky the parents of the boys had chosen not to get the police involved.

"Why didn't you, then?" Ada asked. "You missed an opportunity."

"We don't call the police," Mrs. Guten said. "The parents have to initiate that."

"Thanks for the primer," Ada said. "I'll remember that the next time someone attacks my son."

"Of course they didn't want to press charges," Kevin said. "Would you want everyone in Mungers Mills to know what cowards you were?"

Mrs. Guten repeated that they would investigate Pan's having been bullied, but since he was putting forth no defense, they had no choice but to act on what had been witnessed. He had struck two kids with a tennis racket in plain sight of a bus driver, who had fainted and had to be brought to the emergency room.

Pan told me this is where it got really nasty. Ada turned to Mrs. Guten and said, "This must be very difficult for you. When did you add the *Mrs.* to your name? A safety precaution, clearly."

Pan said that judging by her reaction, Mrs. Guten had not seen that one coming. But despite the booby trap, she and Dr. Jackson were intractable. Pan was suspended for five days. When Ada and Kevin objected, Pan finally broke in, "I'll take the suspension. I just want to get out of this place. I hate it here."

"You can request a superintendent's hearing," Dr. Jackson said.

"No," Pan said. "I don't want to see any more of you."

"We have decided to assign James a home tutor," Mrs. Guten said.

"Yes," said Dr. Jackson. "We're not required by law to do so, since James is seventeen, but in this case we're making an exception."

This patronizing was all Ada needed to fully melt down. She actually got up and started for them. Pan said Mrs. Guten and Dr. Jackson held their heads back like they were watching a hatchet murder. He was awed himself.

"Kevin stopped her with just a touch," Pan said, "but he didn't apologize for her. He said manners were for charm schools. Ada got herself together enough to say they were a unique pair of incompetents. Then we left."

"It sounds horrible."

"For a family outing, not all that unusual. It could only have been better if my real father had shown up to lecture them about political action committees."

"I know I'll never get an answer I can understand," I said, "but why didn't you back up your parents? Why didn't you say something, or let me say something? All those times?"

"I don't know exactly," he said. "I guess I'm like you in a way. I like to keep my humiliations to myself. But it's all over. We're moving."

Chapter 34

As much as I may have cherished things staying safe and static—or sailing side by side—life was suddenly baffling. My best friend was moving. The pharmacy was closing.

Tammie told me about the closing my first night back after the incident, and she insinuated that I had something to do with it. But eventually she let on that the funding for the new residences had not come through, that instead the agency was moving all its people outside of town into fewer, bigger places. Then she grabbed me and hugged me and said, "Nia, I know you'll find another job. It won't be so easy for me."

"You'll find one, Tammie. You will. This was just a stop along the way."

"No, no, I worked my way up to manager here."

I didn't correct her.

She started to cry into my blouse. "That's not going to happen so easy for me again."

I let her weep. I would have expected Tammie's crying to sound like a cat's, but she was almost noiseless.

The pharmacy closing was the prelude for the first real grief of my life, Pan's leaving. I couldn't handle the thought.

Maybe his parents would change their minds and stay. But they all wanted to go. Pan could take his finals, and then it was just a matter of time. Kevin, who had been putting feelers out for awhile anyway, had found a techie job in Brookline, outside of Boston. Their house hadn't sold, but that wasn't stopping them. Pan needed to start fresh again, with a new school record.

"I guess he shouldn't have hit them," Caspar said on the last day of school as we rode in his truck. There was no walking home with Pan anymore.

"That's what I thought at first. That's what I said to him. But didn't they deserve it?"

"They deserved something. But he did the wrong thing. He got himself in trouble instead of them."

"But what else could he do? Really, if he had gone to Guten before, would it have done any good?"

"She could have gotten them suspended. Or something."

"But she would have had to follow him around. She can't keep track of everything that goes on in that school."

"He should have done something else. I really wish he had."

I thought about this. He was right, and yet Pan was, too.

"Cas," I said, "remember how you put Samsonite up against your locker?"

"Yes."

"Well, I know Pan shouldn't have done what he did, but what's the difference?"

It was as close to criticizing him as I'd ever come. Caspar kept driving. His mouth hung open, the look he got when he was transported by thought. He was silent so long that I was sure he was angry and not going to talk to me.

"I think you're right," he said at last. "I hadn't thought of that."

"But, I mean, what you did was fine. I kind of enjoyed seeing Samsonite scared for once."

"The difference between what James did and what I did is that no one saw me. No one who could get me in trouble for it."

I put my hand on the back of his neck, giving him a light massage.

"I could ask myself the same question," he said. "What should I have done instead when he made me mad? Go running to Mrs. Guten? I would have felt like a fool."

"Yeah."

"I'm very sorry to see James go. It happened so quick." He thought for a while. "Anything can change in a second."

"I know. I hate it."

"I'm sorry for your sake, Nia. And mine, too. He was a friend. I don't actually have a lot of friends, as you may have noticed." We sat with that a moment. Then he said, "I wonder if anybody really does."

I could feel loss squeezed in the cab with us, like a hitchhiking ghost. I ran my fingers through Caspar's hair. I was not letting him get away, ever.

"It's not fair," he said. "James shouldn't leave. He shouldn't have to."

The words out loud made Pan's leaving irrevocable.

"No," I whispered. "He shouldn't."

~

The move came fast. There was little time to prepare myself. Pan came to the pharmacy and helped me and Tammie with our final inventory a few times, but I didn't feel the smallest crumb of contentment anymore. Caspar invited us for a pool party of three, which should have been fun. We were listless, though, none of us enjoying the water. Then Caspar suggested what we should have done in the first place.

"Let's have movie night one last time," he said. "Even if it is afternoon."

"We have thousands of titles to choose from," said Pan. And so we went into the cellar on a beautiful summer day.

In the few remaining weeks, Pan and I took some long walks, but my heart was always in my throat. All I could think of was how there wasn't enough time. Also, I was wary of anyone who came near us, who drove by too slowly, even cops, anyone who might be looking for Pan.

At the end of July, he stopped by my house in his mom's car. It was late in the morning, and they were leaving that day. I'd kept hoping for more time, another day or two, but this was it.

Mom had planned to go shopping, but she stayed to say good-bye. Paolo was entranced watching TV from his playpen, for once not interested in Pan. Dad was safely at work.

Pan revealed a narrow, wrapped box and placed it in front of Mom.

"Open it," he said.

The wrapping paper was heavy, with ornate, textured designs.

"You shouldn't," Mom said, her eyes ablaze as she undid each fold as if it were a bird's curled wing. Just as delicately, she pried off the tape.

"Can't a boy give his second mom a present once in a while? Now hurry. I hate surprises."

"No, I want to use the paper again," she said. "Several times." Then she sucked in a long breath. "James, no. I can't."

"You just did," he said with the corner of a smile. The sleek, brushed-steel laptop looked out of context on our enamel table.

"It's too much, no," Mom said. "Take it out of the house this minute. Before I run away with it."

"Nope, it's staying," said Pan. "And it's used, a few months, anyway. Kevin gets new geek toys every six months. He never misses an opportunity to buy himself the latest."

"He does know you're giving this away," I said. "Doesn't he?"

"No, I just took it off his desk. Along with his passport."

Mom was too enchanted to hear.

"There may still be some porn on the C drive, Mom. I can erase it. If you want."

Mom nodded, then lifted the top and touched the power button as if it would open the gates to the mansion.

"Oh, it is beautiful," she said. "We've been talking about getting a new one for years now. Our monitor is the size of a microwave oven. This is perfect."

"Oh, it's also a microwave," said Pan.

"Pan, that's really generous," I said. "Where's my present?"

"She's in the car," he said. "You and Gram will be very happy together."

"Perfect timing, too," said Mom, still fascinated. "I'm getting ready for my next try at school. One course at a time. The advisor suggested I do a class online."

"This baby is so fast you'll need a leash for it," said Pan. "And more storage than a grain silo."

Mom looked up. "No, the first thing I'm going to do is write a letter to that school board about the way they treated you."

But neither of us wanted to go there. We all looked at the laptop, waiting.

Mom broke the silence: "I'm making lunch for us. It's a

special occasion. It's not often I have company bearing gifts."

Pan was right about my mom's cooking. We had pasta with cream sauce and bacon, some green salad, and for dessert, a cake she had made with ricotta and brown sugar. Pan ate like he'd been fasting.

"I'm sending my own mother back here for lessons," he said. "She was driving sixty miles a week to buy natural food, but it's nothing like this."

"We don't care about bugs or chemicals or genetic modifications," I said. "We're a proud people."

"You ought to be. More cake, please."

"You realize, James," Mom said, "that I have no choice but to adopt you. If you won't ever be my son-in-law, you'll just have to be my son."

"Good. I brought the papers for you to sign," he said.

"I'm sure you'd love living in our palace," I said.

"Your château is my château," Pan said, "but I don't think your father would be too happy about it." Defiant little bubbles of joy had risen to the edges of my heart during our lunch. Now Dad, even absent, had popped them all at once.

Mom broke in with a grunt. "Her dad," she said, "is responsible for Paolo. I decide on the next kid." She licked her fork. "Pass me that cake."

She cried when she told Pan good-bye, and he held her like he was leaving her at preschool for the first day. She drove away, swiping at her eyes, waving, then shaking her head. Trying to be strong for Mom had made me feel more able to handle myself.

Pan and I sat on the porch for a while, not talking. I felt like I should say a million things, but nothing seemed important enough.

"I'll write," he said at last. "That's what they say in Caspar's movies, at least."

"No one writes."

"True. But I will call. I'm good at calling. I'll probably call before we've gotten out of Mohegan County, if not sooner."

But the calls would not be the same. He wouldn't be a few miles away, in the same dull town. He would be in Boston, which might as well have been Hawaii.

"You made my mom happy," I said. "Especially with that present."

He put his arm around me. "She would have preferred that you brought out the straight man in me."

"No, she knew that wasn't going to happen. And she wouldn't have liked you if I had. I get the sense my mom doesn't really trust straight guys."

"Your parents are truly a study in opposites."

"Yep."

"Can I get sickeningly sweet for a minute, Nia?"

"You never have before."

"I know. I just want to be gooey this one time. I don't like too many people, and since you're one of the few people I can honestly say I loves, I wanted you to know that I think you may have, on occasion ...."

"Tell me. I'm eventually going to cry no matter what you say."

"Good. I would like quite a lot of mourning. Loud, loud mourning."

"Out with it."

"I just mean, I think you showed me how something works. Kindness. I see it in you all the time and how you don't have to work at it."

"I do love you, Pan," I said, and gulped back a sob.

"Even the part of me that tried to kill two people with a loaded tennis racket?"

"Not so much that part."

"If I had listened to you, I wouldn't be in this mess. What was the point of getting back at those reprobates? They won anyway. No, you always made me think about the right thing to do. I usually ignored you, but you made me think about it."

"It's okay."

"I'm actually kind of sorry we can't be a couple. Just because we would have been so great together."

That made tears shoot out of my eyes almost horizontally. "Don't say that."

"But you have Caspar. And do you know what's deep, deep inside my heart? Way down, past all the bitterness and disparagement and superiority? I'm talking mine-shaft deep."

"What?" I asked.

"I am really happy you found each other."

"Were there drugs in my mom's cake?"

"Could be. But really, I am."

"Yeah?" I tried to breathe normally. "You were nice to him. We had fun, the three of us." Then I blubbered like my ice-cream cone had fallen straight into a dog's mouth. His arm was tight around me. I had to wipe my eyes and nose with the shoulder of my shirt. When that wave of grief pulled back, he relaxed his grip.

I looked at him and he turned his eyes to the sky. "Yeah," he said. He took in a long breath. "He couldn't catch much of a break from me."

He looked back at me, smiling like a comforting grown-up, and petted my hair a few strokes. "He is a good guy, Caspar, as guys go. And he's the only one good enough for my girl."

"You sound like the father of the bride," I managed before another spill of tears.

"That's the toast I'll give when you get married. Should we

promise?"

A second wave was cresting, but I tried to inhale deep enough to fight it.

"Nah, let's not," he said. "Most promises don't age very well. We need an easier one. Let's promise to always remember our almost-year together. The tolerable parts. Oh, and our birthday. Those are easy. Promise?"

"I promise," I said, forcing my voice from the back of my throat. "But I am so afraid."

"Afraid of what?"

"I don't want you to be alone. I don't want anyone to hurt you again and again, like they did here."

"I'll be fine. I always am. Kiss from my best girl?"

"I'm snotty," I said, trying to wipe away the various emissions with my hand.

He tipped my head up with his finger. "You're beautiful. Always were. Always will be." He kissed my cheek. "Loves ya."

"Loves ya," I squeaked.

He got up, moving with his typical grace and rhythm to his mom's car. His beautiful blond hair disappeared inside.

I went back in the house, trying to keep from crying again. I didn't want to inspire Paolo. But he was still sitting in his playpen in front of the TV, mesmerized. He was so still, I thought about getting a hand mirror to check for breath. Then he moved his head and wheezed slightly.

It was risky, but I leaned down and gave him the lightest kiss on the head. He smiled faintly, but didn't stir. I observed his profile. I could already see what he would look like as an old man. His little eyes bulged, his lips were too big, his body was a bowling ball. So what if he was not going to win any cute baby contests? I had enough affection and worry for him to keep him safe.